CHEZ CHANCE

We Find Ourselves in Moontown

CHEZ CHANCE

Jay Gummerman

Pantheon Books
New York

Library of Congress Cataloging-in-Publication Data
Gummerman, Jay.
Chez Chance : a novel / Jay Gummerman.
p.   cm.
ISBN 0-679-43991-9
I. Title.
PS3557.U47C48   1995
813'.54—dc20   95-1731
CIP

Book design by Maura Fadden Rosenthal

Manufactured in the United States of America
First Edition
2   4   6   8   9   7   5   3   1

FOR KELLY

CHEZ CHANCE

‰

It was still bright out, nine hours later, when they landed for the last time and Eastman told the stewardess sitting opposite him not to waste her breath on his account, he would remain seated the rest of his life. She smiled professionally and, he decided, unknowingly, then rose to give her canned speech to the other, enabled passengers who were already moving frantically in the aisles, even though the airplane was still a good distance from the terminal. When she sat down again, Eastman thanked her anyway and asked about a palm tree he was certain he'd seen out the window—just the beginning of a palm tree, he told her, this puny frond of a thing poking from the stretch of dirt between runways—to which she replied, in her professional manner, that this was her first time in Los Angeles, so she didn't know exactly, but she thought palm trees would grow just about anywhere in California.

But by the time he'd parked himself in the terminal, a little flock of flightless birds had concealed the tree from his view, and he watched for a long while from his wheelchair thinking he couldn't be mistaken, as the birds skittered in synch to a steady but unhearable music. Where there were palm trees, there were rats, Eastman reminded himself, and, apparently, little birds, nosing around in the mud for some organism no other creature in its right mind would even think of devouring. Except, of course, for rats. Rats would, and did, eat anything. They were part of the same kingdom as these birds, Eastman thought, the only kind of half-baked life L.A. could support now.

"Feathered rats," he said out loud and smirked, then turned his head to look back over his shoulder as though somebody might actually have overheard him. But everyone else was behind the rope, where they were supposed to be, taking care of their standard airport business. It had been only six months since his accident and already Eastman had learned how to take advantage of his "situation," as his sister, Margaret, referred to it, part of which was authorizing himself into unauthorized places. Margaret thought it was morbid, his wanting to go back to the place where he had fallen, and on vacation no less, but now that he was on permanent disability his whole life was a vacation—he would always be a tourist, even in his hometown—and, besides, his misfortune hadn't changed his primary reason for moving to California in the first place: Missouri winters were insufferable as ever.

Eastman looked again at the birds, who were bracing themselves against what the weatherman on the in-flight broadcast had called rain—a real

drought-buster, he'd called it—but was really a pathetic little mist. It had been *raining* in St. Louis
when he'd gotten on the plane, and it was still raining through the long layover in Denver, thick
droplets the size of bullets. The way Eastman
figured it, people in L.A. would call anything
weather, even the sweat on their iced-tea glasses.
That's why their world was so dangerous, he
thought now, his hand reaching down to scratch
one of his deadened legs, a hangover from his days
of feeling—they had no idea what real trouble was.

Outside, a man and woman in jumpsuits and
headphones were just now preparing to unload the
luggage from the plane. Eastman could tell there
was a thing between them, the way the man strut-
ted around, his long, feathered hair bouncing,
while the woman laughed, exposing her buck-
teeth, at jokes Eastman was sure nobody else
would think were funny. Their flirting escalated as
they passed suitcases to each other, the woman
pretending to drop them, with the man juggling
them on the receiving end. Eventually the woman
reached into the compartment and brought out a

guitar case, which she actually let go of, and the man actually let fall through his hands, onto the rigid tarmac surface. Afterward they looked around slyly to see if anyone had witnessed their carelessness, but they didn't spot Eastman in the window staring down at them, his face shaped in the knowing grimace-smile of an accident victim.

The guitar belonged to the girl in red boots, Eastman was as sure about that as he was the palm tree. He clearly remembered her from the baggage-check line in St. Louis, though he hadn't seen her face: she was small and approximately his own age, which was thirty-four, with red hair and fair skin, and she wore a dress that seemed to Eastman to have been lifted right out of the Dust Bowl, a checkered cotton thing with little straps to hold it on her little shoulders. But the real oddity was her boots—they were cowboy and bright red, the color of lipstick from another era, and when Eastman had looked closer, he saw they were embossed over their entire surface with a tiny icon, what appeared to be Jiminy Cricket singing from the point of a cartoon star. The ticket agent had explained to her that she couldn't carry the guitar onboard the plane, and when she'd told him she was a musician, that her guitar was her livelihood and she couldn't afford to have any harm come to it, a baleful pit boss of a supervisor had stepped up and told her the FAA didn't favor anyone, musicians or otherwise.

Eastman had recognized these people for what they were, the type who would insist on making special provisions for him merely because he was in a wheelchair and thus deprive him of the recently acquired pleasure of holding up the other passengers as he took his time boarding. So he'd hauled his bag to the curb and checked it there, which, as far as Eastman was concerned, was what Red Boots should have done in the first place.

The happy young couple finished with the luggage, and Eastman abandoned his vigil at the window, returning himself to the ranks of the enabled. In Eastman's view the enabled were constantly involving themselves in elaborate behavior they deemed important but that the disabled could see for the mindless distractions they really were. Eastman decided that Red Boots was probably some hybrid of the two, but he couldn't see her anywhere to confirm it—not in the cafeteria or the newsstand or the lounge, where the next round of passengers was busily drinking down their flight insurance. It didn't help that the dress code in L.A. was based almost entirely on flamboyance—in St. Louis he could have seen her boots for miles—but after five minutes or so of looking, he figured she was probably already waiting at the carousel, where her damaged livelihood would shortly be arriving.

He was on his way there himself when he caught sight, at his child's eye level, of her boots underneath a bank of wooden telephone partitions in the center of the lobby. She was seated and swinging her legs—like a little girl at a school assembly, he thought—while everyone in the adjoining booths stood, their bodies, or at least the lower halves, set in the rigid stance of businesspeople. But by the time he'd reached her, it occurred to him he had no idea what he was going to tell her—that she'd been right? that the world really was filled with uncaring assholes?—and when he saw she had her guitar with her after all, he gripped hard the arms of his wheelchair, trying in vain to suppress an enormous blush.

This was the exact moment she swiveled around on her stool to face the airport lobby, the phone still pressed against her ear. Her eyes immediately fell on Eastman, but she didn't look away, as just about everyone did when they saw he was a paraplegic. Instead she seemed to examine him without passing judgment as she listened to whose-ever voice was talking to her on the other end of the line. Maybe she was on hold, Eastman thought, just as he was now, waiting for her to acknowledge his presence. If he'd still had use of his legs, he would have already taken the newly vacated booth next to her and pretended to make his own call. But this was better, he decided—you had to face things when you couldn't run anymore—and in that instant whatever feelings of embarrassment he'd had left him, and he looked at her with what he imagined was her mirror image, his eyes fixed in the same cameralike gaze she had trained on him.

She was the very picture of innocence, with high, cherubic cheekbones atop long-rutted dimples, and eyebrows that never quite lost their arch, as though she were in a state of perpetual amazement; it had been a long time since Eastman had seen a woman his age not wearing any makeup, and he felt relieved, as though he'd been subjected to frauds for so long he'd forgotten what the real thing looked like. There was something not quite formed about her face—her eyes weren't quite blue and they weren't quite aligned either, and her nose and lips seemed to belong to someone much younger. And yet the energy she threw off was too penetrating to be unfocused. It was as if she'd been born prematurely, he thought, but only in terms of her appearance, a trait that was forever causing people to underestimate her and, as a result, indulge in the sweet stickiness of her flytrap.

Eastman caught himself starting to smile at this assessment but pulled back, sensing she had reversed her own reverse psychology on him. He was being conned, he knew that much, though as he stared into her expressionless eyes, he couldn't think into what. In another moment, when he still didn't have an answer, he panicked and looked away, though he could still feel the magnetic pull of her awareness steadily tugging on his being.

Then it occurred to him that he had projected his whole jaded outlook onto this woman, who was, in fact, a perfect stranger—for all he knew she really was an innocent—and when he looked at her again, she was smiling at him, an unselfconscious smile like a child's, as though whatever she was hearing in the receiver was finally in synch with what she was seeing.

"OK, sweetie," she said into the phone, though she might have been saying it to Eastman. It was as if she had all at once recognized him, he thought, as if she'd been expecting him all along. "I'll see you in a little while," she said, turning to hang up the phone, and when she swiveled back, she had a new look about her, though not one Eastman recognized.

"Chance is funny," she said, addressing Eastman exclusively for the first time. "He has one of those walkie-talkies—what do they call them, molecular phones?—and it turns out he's driving around right near here anyway. Chance was a Howard when we were growing up, but he took our mother's maiden name in the eighties, and he hasn't been the same since."

The same as what? Eastman wanted to know, but he felt if he asked her, he might rupture the peculiar mood she had managed to erect around herself. Besides, chance *was* funny, he thought, even if it did happen to be the name of her brother.

"Now he's in real estate," she said, rolling her eyes in an exaggerated manner. "Can you feature that? I don't recollect him ever playing Monopoly when we were kids."

The phone she had just hung up began ringing, but she acted as though she didn't hear it, or anything else for that matter, and they sat staring at each other while the phone droned on and on and on. Eastman was beginning to wonder if she weren't somehow emotionally disturbed when the phone stopped mid-ring and she seemed to remember it was the obligation of normal people to make conversation—not that she, or they, really wanted to.

"I'm Violet, Violet Moonier," she said, and extended her hand, which Eastman took and held for a moment without ever actually shaking it. "Chance calls me Ultra sometimes, on account I'm so much the way I am."

"Frank Eastman," he said, and deliberately left it at that. He wanted to hear some more of her funny—was it antiquated?—way of speaking before he revealed anything more about himself. Maybe he wouldn't have to, he thought—she seemed as if she could carry the whole load by herself.

"Are you a Buddhist?" she asked, and for the briefest of moments she laughed wickedly, in counterpoint to her angelic face. "How do you do, Frank? That's a funny expression, isn't it? 'How do you do?' For the longest time I thought it should be 'Why do you do?' but then it hit me that's what people say when they part company, when they can't figure out what went wrong. Anyway, I don't expect you to answer—how you go about yourself, I mean—it's just a figure of speech. Oh, what am I thinking? You knew that already, didn't you?"

She didn't wait for him to respond, but instead picked up her guitar and began walking down the long corridor toward the entrance of the airport, calling to Eastman over her shoulder, "We'd better get our luggage then."

And he wasn't at all surprised that he followed her immediatcly, wheeling himself as fast as he could just to keep her in his sights; he knew after his accident he'd become a wild card, that he needed to pair up with someone or something or he wouldn't pass back into existence. Even Margaret, who was the opposite of intuitive, had seen it on his face when he'd left for California this time. She hadn't even bothered to ask where he'd be staying or for a phone number where he could be reached—she knew he didn't know himself.

Eastman had marked his sister's apathy as the unofficial end to one of his family's longest-running movies: the dream of moving west. It had always been, as long as he could remember, Margaret's sacred province to speak in her hokey way of California's promised real estate, with a few carefully-spaced negatives thrown in, just so no

one would think she was a left-field religious con-
vert. But as usual, it was Eastman who, despite the
usual protests, had taken action, quitting school
again and actually moving to L.A., where he'd taken
a low-paying job with the phone company. As the
youngest in his family, he had always seen it as his
role to make real what the rest of them could only
imagine, just as it was their role to warn him about
behaving rashly while at the same time secretly
hoping that he would. In this way they hedged
their bets—if things worked out they could follow
in his footsteps, or if things didn't, if he came back
in a wheelchair, like the veteran of some distant
and ill-conceived war, they could nod their heads
with grim faces and rationalize what was left of
their fading pedestrian lives.

It was as if Eastman had robbed his family of its
last article of faith, as if by crippling himself he'd
proven what they couldn't bear to believe all along:
that California really was a congregation of shiny
losers, of people who thought they were superior
and because of it met their cruel fates head-on. In
another month his parents were dead, victims of an

accident themselves—the fuselage from a light air-craft had fallen through their roof, killing them as they slept—and Eastman knew from that day forward his life would be dominated by rabid kittens and stray tires bounding toward him at high speed. There was no point in wading upstream either—that just made your life harder. He would simply let the tide of everydayness take him where it went.

By the time Eastman had caught up with Violet, she was sitting next to the carousel on her suitcase, a huge trussed-up thing with wood showing through its worn canvas cover. She watched Eastman retrieve his bag, then led him outside to the curb, where he supposed they would wait for her brother to collect her. He wondered how far she was willing to go with their business, whatever it was, and if she understood his willingness to go the distance with her. He still wasn't sure about her sanity, or how much of her story was the truth. If, for example, she really did play music for a living, did she sing country-western? And if she did, why wasn't she back in Nashville, instead of L.A., where everything had turned to rap by now? He decided he would let her initiate the conversation again whenever she got around to it. There was no sense in rushing things—that was the purview of the enabled—and he had nothing but time on his hands anyway.

They stared for quite a while at the unceasing parade of cars passing by them, and then she said, "Frank, where are they all going?"

"To Disneyland," he answered, without thinking, and then added, "if you go by their commercial."

"That's where I grew up, did you know that? Well, not *in* Disneyland, nobody grows up there— never-never land and all that—I meant in the neighborhood, we lived a couple blocks away. My father used to maintain all the cars there, the fancy old-fashioned cars they drive around on Main Street to make you feel like you live in some other time. I even got to meet Mr. Disney once."

She seemed to wait for Eastman to comment, but he wasn't sure what she wanted him to say, so he didn't say anything. "I don't think he was a very happy man is all," she went on. "It was like this whole thing he dreamed up one day had gotten away from him, and now it had him by a leash and kept pulling his neck from side to side—like this." She jerked her head around, like someone imitating a chicken, Eastman thought, then laughed when she saw he was watching her so intently. "Anyway, Chance is the last one of us left around these parts—he says he likes everything that's happening, he wouldn't change a thing—but he lives somewhere up in the hills now. You can't even see the Kingdom from there—I asked him that first thing."

Eastman wasn't sure what she meant by "everything," but he decided there was probably no point in asking her about it—her explanation would just confuse things more than they already were. Besides, he saw an aperture, and if he didn't force himself through it right now, he might not get the chance again.

"I'm on vacation," he told her, his face molded into an expression he meant to resemble joy. "It so happens I'm spending the entire week at Disneyland."

She looked directly into his eyes a beat and then stared out again into the evolving traffic. "I'm glad," she told him. "I was beginning to worry you might be homeless. I don't guess they have too many homeless camped out on Tom Sawyer's Island."

"I wouldn't know," Eastman said. "It's my first trip to Disneyland."

Which was true, he had never been, though his onetime roommate, who had been fired there as a teenager, had told him they posted plainclothesmen everywhere, to "weed out unsavory characters," he'd said, between tokes of imported marijuana. Eastman couldn't imagine their being any more tolerant of transients, though he thought it might be worth checking out for himself.

"When did you move back?" he asked Violet, and when she looked puzzled, he said, "East, I mean."

"After I quit Fat Ruby's," she said plainly, as if he should know exactly what she meant. "That was in the days before liquid diets, and I don't think they had those lard vacuums back then either. A masseuse, they called me—I used to rub the fat out of movie stars—or at least I gave it a whirl. I know

I made them feel better about themselves. You'd be surprised how sad famous people get sometimes."

Eastman couldn't tell if she was including herself in that category or not. She didn't talk like any Southern Californian he'd ever known, or, for that matter, anybody he'd met in St. Louis. "Are you a musician?" he asked her, and when she offered him no expression, he rephrased the question, as if he were speaking to someone from another country: "Do you play guitar for a living?"

"What makes you ask that?"

She was looking at him with genuine curiosity now, and he realized he had rushed things after all, despite his best intentions not to. He was still trying to think of an answer when a bright red Mercedes, the color of a fire engine and seemingly of equal power, squealed up to the curb where they were waiting, and a conspicuously fit-looking man in an Italian suit stepped out of its cushiony depths. "Vi," he said, and efficiently hugged Violet, then stooped to pick up her bag, where he came face-to-face with Eastman. This guy was the most enabled person Eastman had ever seen.

"Frank," Violet said, "I'd like you to meet my brother Chance."

Chance greeted Eastman with an open scowl, though it was concealed from his sister's view, then stuck out his free hand, palm down, as though he were reaching for something he knew he shouldn't touch. Eastman watched the hand for a moment and then realized he was meant to shake it—he decided it was in his best interests not to.

"He's staying at Disney's," Violet told her brother. "I thought maybe we could offer him a lift, since we're headed in that direction anyway."

Chance straightened up and, with his back still to Violet, gave Eastman an exasperated look, a look that Eastman interpreted as, You'll have to forgive my sister, she's between planets right now.

"I'd love a ride," Eastman told him, knowing he was expected to politely refuse, then watched as the light flickered out in Chance's eyes. Violet's smile was in direct proportion to her brother's frown, and in that moment Eastman could see the family resemblance, where he hadn't seen one before. He wondered if people still ever thought he looked like Margaret and remembered, after a brief deliberation, that when you sat in a wheelchair, people associated you with other cripples and no one else.

Violet made a big production out of helping him into the car, while Chance sullenly loaded their things in the trunk.

"We'd better get going now," she said, after her brother was seated again behind the wheel. "We've got a long drive ahead of us," she added, and the way she said it, the way her voice trailed off into a sympathetic down tone, Eastman thought she'd included him in her faraway destination.

It was in the early stages of twilight when they finally merged onto the freeway, and no one said anything for the longest time as Chance weaved in and out of traffic, always coming up on another, and it seemed, larger flotilla of cars. It struck Eastman that the roads had swelled considerably in the short time he'd been gone, and everywhere there were signs of new construction underway, though he didn't see many attempts at renovating what was already in existence and badly in need of repair. He looked out his window across the vast, palm-lined neighborhoods that fanned out on all sides of him and thought how they must be filled with enabled people, people who were content to live out their lives without distinction and in utter denial of the calamity that was gathering all around them. This guy Chance was no different, Eastman thought: he, like they, believed you simply had to steer around what got in your path and everything would work out fine. That, in fact, was how success was measured in this place, Eastman had determined, by how well you shut out what was happening in the world outside your own. He had tried explaining this to Margaret when she came to visit him in the hospital after his accident, but she was too busy getting off on the melodrama of the whole situation, *his* situation, to hear anything he had to say.

Eastman snickered angrily at this remembrance and sank back into his seat, where he saw the disembodied eyes of Chance sizing him up in the rearview mirror. The traffic had come to a dead halt, and Eastman could hear Violet humming an old-Irish-sounding melody, above the chorus of engines.

"Where you from, Frank?" Chance asked, his eyes again focused on the traffic ahead of them as the car began to slowly pick up speed.

"St. Louis," Eastman said, deliberately clipping his answer. The less said to the enabled, the better off you were—he had learned that much by now.

"Have you known my sister very long?"

Violet stopped humming. "About nine months," she said, and began again immediately, only this time it was almost singing, she was almost pronouncing words.

"Is that right, Frank? Nine months?"

"Well, maybe it's closer to a year," Violet said. "We met at a Grange breakfast, in Brinktown."

"Can't he answer for himself?" Chance asked. He seemed to be addressing them both simultaneously. "Or does he have more than one handicap?"

"Howard," Violet said, with an amused scorn, then turned around in her seat to face Eastman.

"You'll have to forgive my brother, Frank. I interrupted his supper, and he gets very cranky if he doesn't eat his supper on time."

"It was veal piccata," Chance said, "and I did eat it on time. The real problem, Frank, is really two problems: the first is I have a little sister that floats around this great nation of ours like a spore, landing wherever God sends her, and when you're a spore, apparently there isn't any way of communicating in advance when you'll be dropping in, so you just fall where you may and take your chances. The second problem is really your problem, Frank. Vi has this habit of mistaking roadkill for endangered but living species, which she takes into the home of wherever she's crashing at the moment and then flits off again leaving said roadkill to her host's disposal. So if you're thinking about an extended visit at Chez Chance, I can just pull onto the shoulder and let you out right now. You won't have any problem living off the land—in fact, there's this whole separate freeway eco-system out there. I read all about it in the *Times*."

Chance was still gesturing off to his right, even

though he had stopped talking, and Eastman followed his hand out the window, where a huge, tangled mass of vegetation was vining up an overpass. He didn't see any palm trees, though he decided there were probably a few that hadn't yet reached into the unencumbered air.

"All right now," Violet said, and stared fondly at her brother as if his tirade were some predictable bodily function, like labor pains, that could be ignored until the next violent interval. "I told you, Frank is staying up at Disney's, at the hotel. Aren't you, Frank?"

"That's right, Mr. Moonier," Eastman said, still watching the jungle outside, which they were moving past at a steadily increasing rate. A little sucking up seemed in order here, Eastman thought, especially since his heart was set now, with all their talk, on Disneyland.

"Moonier was my husband," Violet said calmly. "Moonier's soul lives elsewhere now, in parts unknowable. Howard would never have taken *his* name. They didn't get on too well, I'm afraid."

Violet looked over at Chance, whose jaw was

tightening, a reaction she seemed to have fully an-
ticipated. "Someday, if I ever have a son, maybe
he'll call himself Slimp." She cocked her head sideways to face Eastman. "Slimp is *my* maiden name.
Still is Howard's, unless he's changed that one now,
too."

Eastman watched the back of her brother's
neck for any sign of eruption, but he seemed to
have retreated into his previous catatonic state,
where, Eastman hoped, he would remain until they
parted company forever. Violet didn't say anything
more either—what was there to say, really?—and
Eastman fell back into a trance of his own, watching the scenery, what little there was of it, flash on
the screen of his window.

In a little while they were nestled again in grid-
lock, and amid the billboards and power lines and
office buildings, the last burst of sun found a single,
snow-capped mountain poking up, improbably, between them. At first Eastman thought it was a wak-
ing dream, some peculiar crossbreed of the day and
night varieties, but then he realized what he was
seeing was Disneyland, or the first outward sign of

it, and he was immediately struck with how pathetic this imitation Matterhorn looked, especially since he was sure it was more famous by now than the mountain after which it had been modeled. He tried imagining what it must have looked like during Violet's childhood, before the sprawling city had engulfed it and the surrounding land still bore actual fruit, and he decided it probably *was* a spectacular site back then, at least to little children, this huge, permanent circus, as natural an object as any created by God. He wondered now if Violet was seeing it, too, or if she had seen it so many times in her life she couldn't notice it anymore, it was simply a part of her vision. Even so, he thought, there was nothing to prevent him from bringing it back to her attention; Chance shouldn't have any problem with that.

"Am I seeing Disneyland?" Eastman asked, his finger, as he pointed, crossing the boundary between the front and back seats.

"Yes," Violet said quietly, as though admitting some despicable flaw in her own character. "We'll be there very soon."

"I'm glad," Eastman said, "I've been waiting a long time for this."

Chance snickered and pulled out onto the shoulder, flooring the gas pedal until they had reached the next exit. He braked only slightly to negotiate the off ramp, and with the traffic light turning green in front of them, he whipped the car around the corner and into the parking lot of an iridescent fast-food franchise. "I hope they have a part for you," he said, and opened his door, his face covered by a sardonic mask. "They're not real big on walk-ons."

Violet nodded her head. "No, they're not," she told Eastman sincerely, though as he sat in the darkness of the back seat, he couldn't think what they possibly had meant. In another minute Chance unloaded Eastman's suitcase and wheelchair, rudely assisting Eastman into it, while Violet looked on with a blank face as if she had witnessed this same scene so many times she had lost the ability to react to it.

"Find me," she told Eastman, as Chance slammed his door behind him and threw the car into drive. "You'll know where to look," and she said it with such conviction Eastman had trouble not believing her, even after Chance had driven them what must have been miles out of his view.

The tinted halogen streetlamps of Anaheim cast the world before Eastman in the eerie, filtered light of a perpetual sunset—everything was easier to see yet harder to tell apart. A haphazard collection of motels and low-rise hotels, gas stations and coffee shops, had long ago superseded the horizon; in fact, their garish signs were so numerous, no one of them made any sense—they had run together into a huge, illumined billboard that shamelessly promoted chaos.

The whole scene made Eastman wonder where in this landscape the permanent residents lived—there really wasn't much space left for them to occupy, he thought—and when he craned his head upward, to the sky, he saw it was empty, even of stars, there was so much light being reflected back off its surface. So they haven't yet developed

heaven, Eastman thought, and when his eyes
swiveled back to earth again, they came to rest on
a small, unlit municipal sign in the foreground:
DISNEYLAND, it said, with an arrow pointing in the
direction he was aimed.

He began wheeling himself down the sidewalk,
which was difficult with his suitcase balanced on
the arms of his chair, and after fifteen minutes or so
of this, when he still hadn't seen the Disneyland
Hotel, he decided he would do the random thing
and lodge at the next motel he came to. This
turned out to be a place called the Tradewinds,
which Eastman considered one of a de facto chain
of motels, with no official connection but for all
intents and purposes identical, since they were,
every one of them, the by-product of the same
1950s pipe dream. It seemed a haven for palm
trees, both figurative and literal: on the green neon
oasis that surrounded the name; on the doors of
each room above the number; in the planter out
front, with primary-colored spotlights shining up
their fat scaly trunks. A flamingo-tinted neon script
attached to the side of the building spelled out VA-

CANCY, and on the wall preceding this a barely visible NO had been stenciled accidentally by what was once the rest of the script, only because it was less faded than the stucco all around it. Eastman understood why no one had bothered fixing this part of the sign: it had long ago lived out its usefulness. One look at this place and he knew the blue-eyed nuclear families who had come here in droves during the fifties would never be returning.

He wheeled himself under a carport roof where guests could register without getting out of their vehicles, and with his arm fully extended, pushed a button that he wasn't at all sure was still connected to a summoning device. After ten minutes or so of waiting he was about to press the button again when he heard someone in the booth above him and realized he couldn't see, and therefore, couldn't be seen by, the person who had answered his call.

"Down here," Eastman said, and wheeled himself backward into the swath of an amber-colored light that was dangling an assortment of night-flying insects. A sleepy-eyed Persian girl in her early teens stared down at him from behind a shield of bulletproof glass. She was wearing an Orioles base-ball cap and what looked to Eastman like bed-clothes; it was as if he'd wakened her in the middle of the night, he thought, when he knew it couldn't have been much past eight.

"I'd like a room," Eastman said. "Preferably away from the boulevard."

The girl grasped a microphone on one end of a metal gooseneck and flicked a switch at the other. "Twenty dollar," her amplified voice said. She was looking past him now with a soft, detached smile, as if she couldn't conceivably expect him to accept her terms.

"I want it for the week."

The smile sharpened into a smirk for a mo-ment, and then, when she saw he was retrieving his wallet, she looked something up in a dog-eared pamphlet sitting on the counter. "One hundurd dollar," she said, without using the microphone this time, and pushed a registration slip and a pen through a hole at the base of the glass. Eastman filled out the form and passed it back along with a hundred dollars in traveler's checks. The girl scanned the registration briefly, then asked Eastman, "Where are your wheels?"

"Just these," he said, slapping the sides of his chair with his hands, and the girl, without saying anything else, passed him the key to door number six.

All the rooms were dark inside, which, when coupled with the fact there were no cars parked in the lot, made Eastman think he was the only guest. Room number six, like all the others, was just off the pool in the center of the court, only you couldn't really call it a pool anymore—it had been packed full of dirt and planted with night-blooming cactuses whose overwrought perfume couldn't mask some baser, underlying smell that Eastman tried to ignore. When he saw a scrawny white cat peering out at him from the thicket, however, he recognized it undeniably as the odor's source, and then quickly covered the remaining distance to his room, grateful that the key turned easily in the lock. He found the light switch immediately and was pleased to see his room was clean and that there was a TV with a remote control bolted to the nightstand. He turned off the light again and managed to hoist himself onto the bed in darkness, lying for a long time with his head flat against the mattress, listening for other signs of life. All he could hear was the distant swishing of traffic and the sound of his own maddeningly regular breathing. It would be later on, he thought, when the rodents started gnawing in the walls.

In a short while he sat up and reached for the phone, also bolted to the nightstand, and from memory dialed the long sequence of numbers necessary to access his long-distance carrier. After a discordant series of clicks, but before he'd heard any ringing, his sister answered the phone in her inimitable, confused way, as if after all these years of technological advancement, she still didn't trust that people's voices could be carried successfully over wires.

"Hello?"

"Margaret, it's Frank."

"So," she said, trying to adopt Eastman's reserved tone, "you're alive."

"I wouldn't be so sure about that."

"You mean I'm speaking to the spiritual world?"

"Get real," Eastman said. "I'm in L.A."

When she didn't say anything to this, he regretted having been so caustic. "Marg, you sound like you're right in the next room."

"A hospital room or an asylum?"

"I'm all right, OK?" he said, his inflection asking her forgiveness. "Nothing's happened to me. I'm lying in my bed in a motel." He let his head fall back onto the mattress and spoke in a confidential manner: "I'm right around the corner from Disneyland," he said, almost whispering, as if he didn't quite believe it yet himself. "This place is real fifties. I'd send you a postcard, except everything is fastened down around here. I don't think I could pry one loose."

"It's all right, Frank," she said, sounding tired now. "You've never sent me a postcard in your life."

"I could always start."

"Frank," she said, with enough exasperation it was a sentence all by itself. "Maybe I should send *you* a postcard, of the Gateway or Big Muddy, just

to remind you of what you're not missing. That's
the way it should be, I think. People should send
postcards from their boring little lives to strangers
in exotic places."

"I'm not a stranger."

"A hula girl gets a postcard from a housewife in
Kalamazoo showing a table piled with laundry. A
royal guardsman finds a postcard in his box at the
palace of a man mowing his lawn in Racine, Wis-
consin. Do you see what a pleasing concept this is?
All along we've been doing this thing backwards."

"I just wanted to let you know I was all right,
that's all. I didn't want to make a big deal out of
this."

"You weren't in much danger of that."

"I'll let you know when there are further developments"—he paused here waiting for her next
wisecrack—"OK?"

"I'll pick you up at the airport when you decide
to come home, Frank. Otherwise, I'm not sure
what we have to talk about."

"The weather?" Eastman asked, and let the
phone drop into its cradle.

*　　*　　*

Gray morning light had begun seeping under Eastman's eyelids when the voice of a woman, emanating from the next room, wakened him entirely. The voice was deep and matter-of-fact and said things like "I've had it with you" and "That's it, Buddy Boy," with an occasional saw thrown in—"You are what you eat" or "Reap what you sow"—repeated three times quickly at a progressively louder volume. Eastman kept waiting for another voice to respond to this, but he finally gave up, dressing himself in yesterday's clothes and wheeling out of his room into the brightly lit courtyard, where the odor of cooking had suffused the air: garlic and cinnamon and ginger converged harmonically in Eastman's nose, a smell that he at first thought was coming from next door. But when the breeze shifted, he realized the aroma had drifted over from the rooms behind the office, where the Persian girl and her family had no doubt bunkered themselves against the bland cuisine of America. It was then that he noticed the car, a red 1960s sta-

tion wagon with simulated wood siding, the likes
of which he hadn't seen in years, parked now in the
space marked five. He wondered if he had somehow missed it the night before, it seemed like such
a natural part of the landscape, and decided it really could have been parked there since its heyday,
as though the Tradewinds' decline hadn't been
gradual, and her assets on some arbitrary date
thirty years ago had been declared defunct, including whatever belonged to the guests who were
staying there at the time. He heard the woman's
voice again briefly—"Yeah, right, whatever you say,
man"—but he couldn't see inside her room; the
window was covered by drapes that, at least on the
outside, bore a print of Snow White and the Seven
Dwarfs happily whistling as they worked at some
undefined task. He sat for a while and tried to hear
more, but it was useless with the soundtrack of rush
hour making short, harsh echoes against the courtyard walls, so he rolled himself onto the sidewalk
and began the final leg of his trip to Disneyland.

By day the signs of the city, which had been so
stubbornly animated in their native darkness, now

seemed spent and fossilized, like a field of wild-flowers gone abruptly to seed and then doused with lacquer. What little chance of rain there had been had dwindled entirely; the sun beat down without hindrance of clouds, and Eastman knew the day, despite what the TV weathermen were forecasting as beautiful, would in truth be oppressively hot and smoggy.

Eastman found the sidewalk practically empty of pedestrians, except for a few isolated street people holding crudely written placards, all of which failed to mark the existence of their authors: FAMILY NEEDS YOUR HELP AND PRAYERS; UNABLE TO FIND WORK; HAVE CONSTRUCTION EXPERIENCE. One woman, whose small child seemed well practiced and perfectly content at scrawling cave drawings on the sidewalk with a piece of Day-Glo orange chalk, had dispensed with all unnecessary verbiage; she had two signs—one simply said, FOOD, the other, MONEY—which she alternated according to some long-internalized scheme. Eastman wanted to tell her that she should add a sign that said LOVE, since she was just as likely to receive that, but he suspected she, like the others, didn't need his advice—they had already mastered failure, which explained why they were here to begin with. He didn't understand how they kept themselves afloat—they couldn't, after all, have selected a more distracted audience for their begging—or why they would even want to. Then he realized that this was their ultimate failure, *the* ultimate failure—not knowing when your life had lost all purpose, so you could put yourself out of your own indelible misery. They were proof that your body could live for years by sheer reflex alone, he thought, long after your soul had traveled elsewhere.

Eastman turned the corner with the rest of the cars, and he was at the gates of Disneyland, or the parking lot of Disneyland, which spread out like an oil slick as far as he could see. He managed to squeeze himself in between a white Cadillac with Nebraska plates that honked at him exactly once and a carload of pan-faced children who stared at him unflinching, even when he waved. In a short while, the parking attendant—when she saw that Eastman's vehicle was, in fact, a wheelchair—said something into a walkie-talkie and then, embarrassed, waved him through, and in another twenty minutes, once he'd spanned the great asphalt sea in front of him, he was being ushered by an unctuous teenaged employee through a turnstileless gate into what his ticket dubbed "The Happiest Place on Earth."

The park at first seemed festive. There were huge banks of flowers everywhere, and the piped-in music, a kind of alpine shuffle, actually lifted Eastman's spirits somewhat, even though he didn't want them to be. A Pavlovian smile accompanied every near–life-size replica of a steam locomotive or castle he came upon, and before the smile could decay entirely, the next attraction would superimpose a new smile over the remains of the last. But at some point Eastman grew tired of it all; he saw now that the robots of pirates and presidents and macaws were programmed with the same spastic caricature of life, and he began to search out the few living inhabitants, other than the burgeoning flock of enabled patrons, that managed to survive in the park—the sparrows and dragonflies and the occasional swan, drifting warily through the littered moats. He was sure there were rats—by the thousands, he figured—but he was also sure that Disney must have assembled a crew dedicated exclusively to their eradication. Rats were quick studies, Eastman knew that much about them, and it was clear they had learned what they were up against; by now they would only show themselves at night, he thought, long after the sapiens had slunk back inside their caves.

By late afternoon the place had become so crowded, Eastman gravitated to the oldest, least popular rides, the ones based on the Disneyfied versions of Grimm's fairy tales—Snow White and Sleeping Beauty and Cinderella—where a minority of small children and their parents, and mostly sarcastic teenagers, had assembled. He felt compelled to test boundaries: on a remote corner of Tom Sawyer's Island; at a vaudeville of mechanical grizzly bears; during a seven-minute round trip to Mars—but each of his attempts at getting behind the scenes was met by a well-rehearsed security official in thematic Disneyland attire who quietly steered him back in bounds.

Eventually he took refuge in the petting zoo;
here a listless bunch of farmyard animals was being
relentlessly pummeled and sat on by enabled children, and when Eastman asked an employee
dressed in overalls and straw hat how he might ac-
quire some of the tranquilizers they used on the
goats, he was told to mind his own business if he
wanted to stay in the park much longer.

His one motivation for staying now was to see
how long he could hide after closing, and with that
not happening until midnight, the idea of enduring
another eight hours of enforced happiness put him
over the edge; he told the agrarian Mouseketeer he
would meet him in Tomorrowland or hell, which-
ever came first, and wheeled himself back to the
Tradewinds.

The next morning was a Sunday, though Eastman received the same wake-up call he had the day
before, the same one-way conversation, spilling—it
would seem involuntarily—from the mouth of the
woman whose existence passed in room number

five. This time he stayed in bed and watched television, all of it in languages other than English: an earnest Korean newscast; a Mexican audience-participation show presided over by an Anglo-ized blonde; a dubbed version of "Lassie," with the husk of June Lockhart crudely inhabited by a staccato, foreign presence that spoke in a tongue Eastman was never quite able to put his finger on. What he realized afterward, with a profound sense of melancholy, was that TV had the exact same effect whether you understood the words or not.

Around noon someone knocked on the door: it was the Persian girl wanting to know if she could change the linens. Eastman switched places with her, easing himself into the exorbitant daylight of the courtyard, where the station wagon remained the only car. He wheeled himself into the organ-shaped pool of earth at the center of the courtyard and closed his eyes, hoping, as the sun penetrated him and prevented him from a very convincing darkness, that the next omen—not even an omen, necessarily, the next prompt—would steer him in another, more fruitful direction. Last night he had dreamt that the Persian girl, dressed in a powder blue haik, had invited him into her kitchen, only it wasn't her kitchen, it was his grandmother's, with its soft, remembered light and white porcelain range. Eastman was a child in the dream, or his spirit was—his body was fully mature and functional, though there was nothing in the least bit sexual about it. The girl had merely told him pleasant, grandmotherly things, things that literally made no sense to him now, but in the dream he had found coherent and soothing. At the moment, the girl was sitting with her back to him, at the table where his grandmother would have rolled out a piecrust, making little mounds of spices he had never seen before, all the while spouting her jovial non sequiturs. He went furtively to the stove and lifted the lid on the pot she had boiling there and saw rats inside, plump drowned rats, sitting at the bottom of the pot, their fur and everything else about them still intact, except for their tails, which had detached and floated to the surface. *"How's the water?"* the girl asked, leaning over his shoulder, only her voice had dropped to a flat and nasal register. Eastman opened his eyes and was looking into the pale face of a surprisingly bland-looking teenager—he could have been one of the attendants from the day before, he thought—smiling his bland attendant's smile. "I said, 'How's the water, dude?'" the teenager repeated in a louder voice, and Eastman understood that the dream had rewritten itself to incorporate the capricious details of reality.

"I was thinking of taking a dip later myself," the teenager said, and stood up, his face suddenly contorted into a different smile, this one composed of several, conflicting emotions. He turned and flashed the smile at a sun-roasted man in roped-on sunglasses and halfhearted dreadlocks who was standing barefoot behind him. But the man didn't return the smile—in truth, he didn't seem capable of it—and the teenager turned to face Eastman again, though without really facing him; he was staring directly over Eastman's head. "I want some of *this* dude's tickets," he said, pointing at Eastman, who looked where the teenager was looking and saw a great ovoid woman, with what appeared to be welder's goggles pushed up onto her nappy blond hair, sitting on a cushioned milk crate in front of door number five. She had managed to locate—or perhaps it was the other way around—the one shadow in the entire courtyard large enough to accommodate her. "Come on, Beatrice," the teenager said, "you giving all the good shit to the tourists now?"

The woman shot a look out of her voluminous face that moved the teenager to silence, and just then the Persian girl emerged again from Eastman's room with a look of her own, a look that in its second-long duration linked Eastman with whatever business was being transacted here, a look of insight and revulsion and grudgingly willful ignorance.

With great effort the egg woman rotated her weight to a standing position, and wordlessly the teenager and his henchman followed her into her room, the door swinging shut behind them. Eastman stayed in the courtyard a while longer, adjusting to the atmosphere that had suddenly fallen over him, and in that short time endured several abbreviated stares from between the Snow White curtains, all, he thought, from the dreadlocked zombie.

Eventually the sun's effects siphoned off Eastman's curiosity, and he returned to his room,
knowing only that something illegal was transpiring without knowing any of the particulars. He
was tempted to call Margaret, but he decided he
couldn't very well explain what had just happened
to him, so he kept a watch of his own, returning
periodically to the courtyard until the heat got to
him again and then moving back inside to cool off.

On each of his visits, he got a better look at the
egg woman, who sat like a toad on her milk crate,
waiting for the flies to come to her. Except for her
weight, there was nothing unusual about her—she
was simply of a larger scale than her associates,
who were, five or six of them in all, average-looking
white kids—younger versions of his former roommate, Eastman thought, kids on the verge of being
fired from Disneyland, if they hadn't been already.
Like the first teenager, each of them made reference to tickets—"I need two tickets"; "Who's got
tickets?"; "Ticket me!"—and each was given a brief
tour of the egg woman's room, appearing afterward with seemingly nothing more than he started.

In between transactions the woman steadfastly re-
fused to make contact of any kind with Eastman,
even when at one point he looked directly into her
eyes for what felt like an hour. This disavowal of
him became increasingly difficult to maintain as
Eastman moved a few feet closer with each new
visit, until finally, when the sun had fallen behind
the horizon of buildings, he stationed himself right
outside his door, directly across from her.

At this close range he watched her without
self-consciousness (he felt they had already been
acquainted, by default), noting that each of her
breaths was a genuine chore for her. Maybe breathing really was as good an accomplishment as you
could expect in such a place, he decided; if she had
belonged to any other species, she would have long
ago been torn apart by coyotes and buzzards—and,
for that matter, rats—but in the contrived domain
of the enabled, she, like Eastman himself, had
merely been dropped from the script.

At last, without looking at him, she said, "What
are you on, anyway?" as if she were joining a conversation already in progress.

Eastman thought about this for a moment. "Vacation," he told her.

She scoffed weirdly, in the manner of an agitated parrot. "You're not on vacation, you *are* vacation. You're the spot after everybody leaves." She was shaking her head. "You don't want anything, man. If you were here, you'd want something. Everybody wants *something*."

"I want tickets."

"So you want tickets. Everybody wants tickets, all right. Standing room only and you bring a frigging chair."

"The chair brought me," Eastman said. "Before that it was a car, and before that an airplane."

"And before that your mama. I know. Your mama brings you into this world and she don't even breast-feed you. It's a cryin shame is what it is. What kind of tickets you lookin for?"

"I haven't decided."

"What do you want, brochures? I guess I must look like a frigging travel agent."

"As much as anything else."

"I am a travel agent," she said. "You want to

leave the planet for a few hours, I can arrange that. I don't deal in specific destinations. Anywhere but here, that's all I guarantee. Usually that's all my customers expect."

"I've already done my traveling," Eastman said.

"You want a ticket home, then, is that it? Join the frigging club, man. But before you split, I've got a question for you: If home is so frigging good, what are you doin here?" She paused as if she actually expected him to answer. When he didn't, she made the parrot noise again. "You ask me, home is where your ass is. And yours is definitely parked where you're already at."

For the first time she looked at him, with an "Am I right?" expression on her face, and when he couldn't think of how to respond, she took this as license to continue her spiel unfettered: "Cash is definitely a factor. So is mileage. There's a whole lot of salt water between here and Polly-nesia, and last time I checked, you couldn't get there by wheelchair. Now, according to my voices, you're paid up for the week and you've already done the Kingdom, so you got nothin but time on your hands, which is fortunate for you because all the good rides are out here anyway. What I'm selling is indoor transportation. The boat inside. You go farther and you pay a lot less."

She kept her eyes fixed on him, waiting aggressively for a reaction, while she noisily ingested the uncensored air all around them.

"You're quite a salesman," he said finally.

She turned her head to face the courtyard again. "Don't have to sell anything," she said. "The product does its own selling."

"I believe you," he said. "I really do."

"You know where to find me," she told him, and withdrew back into herself, and Eastman decided she would stay that way until the next fly had landed within reach of her prodigious tongue.

In the morning when Eastman woke up, the television was still going: an older, nearing-the-end-of-his-career newsman was giving the weather in a bow tie, and he seemed to be looking for assurances from the unblinking lens of the camera that he was still, after all these years, doing all right.

Eastman turned off the TV and listened for the egg woman's morning lecture from next door, but he couldn't hear anything, so he moved outside where the sun was already unyielding—another gorgeous day, as the weatherman had put it—and the egg woman was already conducting business from her pulpit on the milk crate. Her client was the dreadlocked zombie from the day before, and whatever she had just told him registered not on his face, which maintained its single expression, a kind of preemptive sneer, but in his legs—he walked, or rather slow-bounced, out of the court-yard and into the street beyond, without making the usual side trip to the egg woman's room.

"Earthling has the opposite problem," she said, again without greeting or even looking at East-man—salutations seemed to be an extravagance she had trimmed from all her conversations. "He knows what he wants, but his funding dried up a long time ago. Now he fishes any way he can. Last time he got bagged for wearing a Goofy suit. Really it was just the ears, these two flaps of cardboard he colored black and tied around his head. I told him, 'Earthling, you can't wear that shit, Disney's got that shit copyrighted.' But he wore it anyway, tried to sell balloons dressed up like that. They weren't even shaped like Mickey."

She looked at Eastman with what amounted to a glint in her eye, though in any other person he would have called it a glitch. "Maybe I should introduce you two," she said. "I might actually get one whole customer out of it." She glanced around as if she were about to share a confidence. "Just don't let his viny head too close to yours," she told him.

"Who's Earthling?" Eastman asked, wanting her to have to explain more, just to keep her off balance. When she didn't answer right away, he figured she had sensed, then rejected, his motive for asking.

"Earthling's my oldest customer," she replied in time, after he had given up any hope of a response. "The others just disappear after a while—though I wouldn't say Earthling is very *here* anymore. The rest call him RV—that stands for Rastaman Vibration. He's more vibe than person. But he's also a recreational vehicle—Earthling burns up more fuel than anybody I ever done business with. He's seen some shit God didn't want him to see and now he wants to see more of it. You know, behind the curtains where that Oz dude sits."

"Why do you call him Earthling then?"

She looked at Eastman with disbelief—naïveté, apparently, was the only thing that could still shock her—then pulled her goggles down over her eyes. "Because he belongs so much to this earth," she said and folded her arms across the ledge of her stomach. "At least the way they got it set up now."

He looked at her for quite a while after this, hoping futilely that she might elaborate. Instead she began to yawn and speak at the same time, a mixture that sounded like a convoluted strain of whimpering: "You got more questions, you better start dispensing green."

"I thought talk was cheap."

"Cheap, maybe," she said, "but not free. Everything around here has its price. You'll figure that out sooner than later."

"I'll take that under advisement," Eastman said and when she didn't say anything else, he wheeled himself, with the help of her goggled stare, along Earthling's path to the street.

At the McDonald's, Eastman was the only sit-down customer; the rest were queued up in the drive-thru lane, many of them alone and sour-faced and in four-wheel-drive vehicles, as if none of the thousands of paved roads in the area had taken them where they really wanted to go. Eastman sat in a corner booth trying to read a discarded newspaper from the day before, but his eyes kept straying to the new and sparsely planted beds outside, where hundreds of immense Asian cockroaches writhed indefinitely under the fate of slow-acting poison. Ultimately he solved the problem by moving away from the windows and into the center of the restaurant, though when he shut his eyes, their afterimage still lingered, only in reverse: burning white cockroaches squirmed against the flat black background of his mind.

And then he found her, just when he'd forgotten he might actually be looking for something: WITH SPECIAL GUEST VIOLET MOONIER, and above this, the name of the featured performer, a band called Squirreltooth Alice, which was apparently on a reunion tour, though Eastman had never heard of them—it was an advertisement for a nightclub called the Lasso. Violet was playing a two-night engagement there, tonight being her last performance, and though the place was all the way in San Juan Capistrano, Eastman was determined to see her, though he didn't guess it would take six hours and five buses, including two with frozen squatting mechanisms that were unable to lift him aboard.

Even still, the doors to the Lasso were just opening when Eastman finally arrived, though instead of being located in the historic district along with the mission as he had expected, it was actually sited a few miles farther south, in a new and vaguely Spanish-style business park that was visible from the freeway. On one side of it was a tile outlet and on the other a plumbing-fixture showroom, and yet somehow—maybe, Eastman thought, it was just that they shared the same tile-roofed façades—the Lasso managed to fit in, as though the bluegrass instruments featured in the showcase out front had become standard equipment in the new housing tracts shooting up all over this part of the county.

The inside of the building had the same generic atmosphere; the light was gray without being dim and cast evenly over row upon row of long cafeteria-style tables. Eastman looked up and saw several banks of fluorescent bulbs exciting their gas from beneath the high, unbowed ceiling before the usher hurried him to a chairless and otherwise empty pen near the front of the enabled area.

Eastman situated himself off to the side of the stage where he didn't think Violet would notice him, and when she did at last come on, unaccompanied except for her guitar, it was an hour after the posted show time, after the audience of suburban cowboys and cowgirls had been served their two-drink minimum and the general mood in the place had become more like one preceding a bullfight.

She was wearing the same dress and red boots

she had worn that day in the airport, and she still wasn't wearing any makeup, a fact vulgarized by the shaft of compressed glare that instantly enclosed her once she'd gotten up onstage. She was more of a specimen than a performer, Eastman decided, an exotic species extracted from the deep— of momentary interest, but not really what her captors were after, and so left to die in the sun.

She stood exposed for a minute or two before a thin, unmodulated voice finally announced her over the P.A., and without adding anything more of her own, she broke immediately into song. But clearly her moment had passed: her singing voice, which was a high, exaggerated twang, hovered above the audience for a few bars before it sank below the undistinguished voices that had already filled the room again, and it stayed there as it put forth laments and spirituals and songs of pastoral and life-ending love, of a world she could know nothing about, except by secondhand, or from the mouths of long-dead relatives.

At first Eastman thought she was kidding, but the strained and nasal voicings, the predictable and maudlin lyrics, were all delivered with the same perfectly straight face; it was as though she were doing a poor imitation of a hillbilly, he thought, an image that had little, if any, basis in fact, but had existed for so long and in such number in various media that it now passed for a peculiarly false kind of truth.

As he watched her, Eastman wasn't at all sure if she was aware of her own affectations, if she knew that her accent sounded patently fake or that her appearance was out-of-place, and just when he'd decided that this was her only way of expressing her version of things—it didn't matter what she knew or didn't know about herself—she began a song about a town, a place where everybody was leaving or had already left, and the woman who was telling the story recounted her uneventful life there and by the end of the song was leaving now too—only there was nobody to hear her, she was saying goodbye to a place that had become hers alone, a place that was already empty.

When she finished the song, Eastman broke into spontaneous applause, though when he was done clapping, he noticed that most of the audience, who before were indifferent, were now making impatient rumblings. And the ruder they got, the more Violet twanged, and the more Violet twanged, the ruder they got, until people were shouting sarcastic things at the stage, all of which Violet abided with her angel's persona. Eastman couldn't tell if she was behaving out of neurosis or spite—he suspected a little of each—though it was clear she had spent a good part of her life performing for hostile audiences, both on and off the stage.

A square-jawed bouncer appeared behind Violet just as she was finishing her last song, a particularly drawn-out version of "Will the Circle Be Unbroken," and as he escorted her offstage, a woman near Eastman with spun hair dyed the color of tarnish yelled out, "So long, Gomer," and the other hecklers in the audience, fully in concert now, erupted in laughter. Only then did it occur to Eastman that these patrons of the Lasso, in their cowboy hats and silver-tipped Western array, considered themselves the real thing, unlike the interloper on stage, who qualified in their minds as a relic of romanticized history. He wondered if he had participated in such lynchings when he was still a member of the enabled, and decided, with a fair amount of regret, that he probably had.

After Violet he couldn't bear to sit through Squirreltooth Alice, so he waited in the little walled-in parking lot behind the building, in the darkroom orangeness of the security lights, through the band's amplified paces and the intermission and Violet's second act, of which he could thankfully only hear snippets.

Somewhere in the middle of the next break Violet stepped out of an emergency exit on the side of the building, releasing for a moment the hostile spirits inside before the door swung closed to seal them up again. With guitar in hand, she began walking briskly in Eastman's direction, her mouth crimped in the same tinny smile she had worn onstage, a smile, he thought, that would take hours to flatten out again, it had been held so long in its one position. As she approached, he saw she was looking past him, her eyes, as they had been during her performance, fixed on a point forever in the distance, but she stopped as she was just about to eclipse him, her face seeming to try on five or six disguises before it found the right one—in this case, a look of exhausted, though unfailing, generosity.

"Can I give you a lift someplace?" she asked, but before he could answer, she had already walked past him, and by the time he had wrenched his chair around, her guitar was on the asphalt by her side and she was aiming something at an early-model Cadillac, bearing the license plate SELL HI, that was parked directly in front of her. Eastman heard a sound like two quick swipes of a squeegee, only higher-pitched, and Violet went to the passenger side of the car and tentatively turned the key in the lock, as if it might at any moment deliver a lethal electric current. When nothing happened, she opened the door and the car began issuing a series of different cartoon noises—whoopings, buzzings, slide whistles—repeated over and over in the same sequence like the song from an electronic mockingbird. Eventually Violet squeezed the right button and the noises stopped, and then she quickly beckoned Eastman with her hand, as though she thought if they hurried, they could somehow avoid a similar, cacophonous fate. This turned out to be her last communication until they were on the freeway headed back toward Disneyland.

"Sometimes I feel naked when I'm not in a car," she told him, and smiled—an actual smile, Eastman thought—while her eyes darted between the rear- and side-view mirrors. "Especially when I come back home."

"I never feel naked," Eastman said. "Even when I'm naked."

She started to change lanes, without signaling or looking over her shoulder, and almost hit a passing sports car, which honked and swerved into the far left lane before rapidly speeding out of sight. "That's too bad," she said, and he wasn't sure if she was talking about him or her failure to involve them in an accident. Then she took her eyes off the road a moment to look at him. "It's good to feel naked sometimes, don't you think?"

"Do you feel like the audience is naked?" he

asked her quickly, before she could look out the windshield again. "That's what they always told us in speech class—imagine that the audience is naked. I always thought that if they were I'd be a lot more nervous than if they weren't. Who knows what a naked audience means? The whole concept scares the hell out of me."

He was surprised that he had said so much, and he could tell by the look on her face, a kind of dazed grin, that she was, too.

"It means you're playing to a convention of naked people," she said thoughtfully. "The delegates of nakedness are rooting you on in all your glory."

She slowed the car to a speed well beneath the limit and pushed a button on the dashboard, then adjusted a dial until it was completely dark inside the car—even the speedometer was invisible—and leaned back in her seat with her fingers barely touching the wheel. "Chance owns four cars," she said. "But this is the only one that has a cruise control I can work."

"Is that why you drive this one?"

"He won't let me drive any of the others. I think it's because they're all new." She glanced over at Eastman, who was looking right at her, and then back at the freeway. "I told him I was going to the movies tonight, and he said, 'Which one?' and I said, 'I don't know, I'll choose when I get there,' and he said, 'Where's it showing?' and I said, 'The mall,' and before he could ask, 'Which mall?' I picked up my guitar and beat it out of there."

"So he doesn't know you're a singer."

"He knows I'm a singer all right. He just doesn't know I get paid for it is all."

"Why don't you tell him?"

"I know he'd be disappointed," she said, and looked genuinely sad, in the time it took the head-lights from a passing truck to shine in and out of the car. "He has ideas about the world. People like me aren't supposed to be able to exist in it. For all I know, he could be right." She paused, and he could feel her look at him in their little bubble of darkness. "He still gets angry when I talk at him, though. I don't guess a spook would have the same effect. He wasn't like that when we were kids—he used to sing right along with me in church. I don't know. When he got older he decided he couldn't change things to what he wanted them to be. Then he started hating himself for ever thinking that he could."

She didn't add anything else, which after several miles caused Eastman to wonder if she was beginning to doze behind the wheel. His body had just started tensing into a familiar panic when he saw in his peripheral vision a little oasis of palm trees growing out of the ice plant on the side of the freeway, in the ecosystem Chance had read all about in the newspaper.

"Spooks don't have any effect," he said, as much to break the spell as anything else. "They're stuck watching people make the same idiot mistakes that got them turned into spooks." He could tell she was smiling, though he wasn't sure through which one of his senses. "Take palm trees. I never thought much about palm trees until my accident. It's not like they were this big symbol to me or anything. Palm trees were what they painted on the set when Hope and Crosby went out on the road."

He looked over at Violet's silhouetted profile—
he just knew she was smiling—then out through
the windshield along with her. "Now I see them
everywhere. *Washingtonia filifera.* They don't bear
coconuts, did you know that? They're a different
breed entirely. *Washingtonia* bear rats. That's pretty
funny isn't it, rat-bearing palm trees?"

"Are you saying you're a spook, Frank?"

He wondered now, as the subdued lights of the
suburbs gave way to the first, gaudier versions of
the city, if she had absorbed any of what he'd just
told her. "Maybe I'm just spooky," he said.

She let a finger slide down his arm. "I can touch
you," she told him. "You can't be too spooky."

"You don't know anything about me," he said
angrily. "I'm just some guy you picked up in the airport. I could be a practicing cannibal for all you
know."

"I can't say I've ever known one of those," she
said, with enough rue to imply she longed for the
experience.

"You think I'm harmless because I'm in this
fucking chair. If I could still walk, none of this

would be happening. You wouldn't have offered me a ride, and I wouldn't have taken you up on it even if you had. What we're experiencing now is a fluke, a random sequence of events. Somebody spliced together all of God's little outtakes and now they're playing it back. There isn't any fucking script."

"That's it, Frank," she said, "get it out of your system."

"I'm not angry," he told her. "I'm way past that. Denial's first. Then comes anger, then bargaining, then depression. Acceptance comes last. It's all in the book my physical therapist gave me. For the longest time I didn't think about who that book was aimed at, even though it was right there on the cover. Such are the powers of denial. But at some point in my depression the picture got a whole lot clearer. Do you know who that book's written for?"

"Yes," she said.

"The terminally ill. The terminally *fucking* ill. The only problem was, in the book, the hero makes his own funeral arrangements and then the screen goes black. But in my case—well—there's no de-

scription of the next fucking stage. What's after acceptance, that's what I want to know? Nobody
ever bothers answering *that* fucking question."

"God's little outtakes," she stated flatly. "You
want to get something to eat?"

"Why not?" he said, used now to her oblivion,
and she pulled off the freeway into the eddy of ad-
vertising mantras that he recognized as the neighborhood surrounding Disneyland. With all of the
signs, Violet was lit up again, and he watched her as
she calmly picked her way through traffic humming a dirgeful tune, what sounded to Eastman
like "The Streets of Laredo." When she hit her first
red light, she stopped humming and smiled, and
then seemed to remember someone else was in the
car with her. "It's hard to get a word in edgewise,"
she said, her eyes wide and seemingly lidless, as if
they belonged to a trout. "What with all the pitch-
ing going on, I mean."

She let her gaze drift out the window, and Eastman followed it, watching it settle on a middle-
aged panhandler and a religious pamphleteer, who
stood waiting together in the concocted light. They

were two distinct species, Eastman decided, like a squirrel and a pigeon, hoping for the same few, reluctant alms.

"I'd never heard that about palm trees," Violet said as the light went green. "They had a lot of them out in Indio where my grandfolks lived. Date palms, I believe they were. Do you think they bear rats, too?"

"Probably," Eastman said, and saw their reflection for a moment in the mirrored window of a saloon—they looked like a pair of renegade children, he thought. "But I won't be climbing any more ladders to find out."

"Was that your job," she asked, "picking rats?" and then she laughed the same wicked laugh he remembered her using briefly in the airport.

"I trimmed trees for the phone company," he said, a little stunned by her laughter. "They warned me about the rats, but I guess I thought I'd be ready for them. I didn't figure they'd jump out at me." He shook his head. "The rats were a surprise, all right. And it wasn't even my birthday."

He looked down at his atrophied legs and remembered how after his accident he would pound them with his fists until he thought he would pass out from exhaustion. He supposed now that he'd been somewhere between denial and anger at that point in his life, which, really, when he thought about it, wasn't very long in the past.

Violet pulled the Cadillac into the lot of what looked like a coffee shop—ANTOINETTE'S, it said on a large oval can sign that was slowly turning on the roof, though without explaining what it was of such monumental importance that Antoinette possessed—and managed to fit the car into the remains of the parking space between two nearly identical vans. There would be enough room—barely—for Eastman to set up his chair, but Violet had to crawl out on Eastman's side, she was parked so close on her own.

"The House of Big Food," Violet announced, after she had reached the heavy glass doors of Antoinette's and opened one of them for Eastman to enter. But Eastman was preoccupied with a red station wagon, parked in the handicapped spot by the entrance, which, except for a disabled license clearly visible in the windshield, was the spitting image of the one he had seen parked at the Tradewinds. It seemed inconceivable that there could be two cars like it within the same square mile, let alone the rest of Southern California, though Eastman figured he would know soon enough if the egg woman was indeed inside the restaurant.

"They should hire me as a doorman," Violet said, and Eastman, taking the hint, wheeled himself into the low-ceilinged interior of Antoinette's, where a large Ethel Merman-like woman in a floral-printed muumuu and go-aheads had propped herself with the aid of a metal stool against a wall papered by business cards. Eastman decided that the woman was more sentry than hostess, though he couldn't think of what in such a tacky place like Antoinette's would be worth guarding.

"How many?" the woman asked, knowing that the answer was two, but wanting Violet to have to say it anyway, a perversion Eastman recognized as if it were one of his own. Her heavily lip-sticked mouth appeared to naturally rest in a smirk, which, when matched with her unsullied blue eyes, made Eastman think she was genetically ironic.

"Guess," Violet said, and the woman, without altering her expression, took up two gargantuan menus in her meaty hands and slipped off her stool, leading them in her stylized slowness past a mirrored display case filled with gargantuan replicas of food—a cheeseburger the size of a wheelbarrow tire, with an actual wheelbarrow tire sitting next to it for reference; a tapioca pudding in a spittoon-size goblet; a platter piled high with spaghetti and meatballs, and stuck in its summit, a flag on a swizzle-stick pole that said ON TOP OF OLD SMOKY!—to a green Naugahyde booth, near the front of the restaurant, of surprisingly modest proportions.

Violet excused herself to go to the bathroom and was forced to travel in the torpid wake of the hostess as she plodded back to her station, which afforded Eastman the opportunity to scan the restaurant for the egg woman. He realized, however, after looking around for a minute or two, that spotting her wouldn't be as easy as he'd first thought: Antoinette's was filled for the most part with people who, like the egg woman, had ignored the surgeon general's warnings on fat intake over the last twenty years; everywhere he saw obese and near-obese people calmly masticating enormous steaks and mammoth helpings of fries of one sort or another, all with the same benign expression on their faces, as if—as was apparently the case—there was nothing unusual about the expanse of their meals.

At the opposite end of the restaurant, Eastman saw a gaunt, well-, though not formally, dressed young man of Asian descent sitting by himself, his hands perched on the handles of an urn filled with some hot beverage whose steam was rising, unrefracted, through his pensive gaze. The only other aberration was a group of teenagers sitting at a table near the cigarette machine—they might have been out of Depression-era movies, Eastman thought, in their baggy clothes and schoolboy hair slung with Kangol caps—who were staring transfixed as the diners all around them devoured their heaping portions. It was only when one of them jabbed another sitting next to him who burst spontaneously into red-faced laughter that Eastman realized they were here not to dine themselves, but to witness the freak-show aspect of the proceedings. Now he understood why the hostess had viewed him and Violet so skeptically: they, like the teenagers, belonged to the prevailing order—at least in the world outside of Antoinette's—of thin people.

Eastman still hadn't spotted the egg woman by the time Violet, who seemed fully decompressed now, eased down into the booth and smiled over at him. She could do the talking for a while, he thought—just as he had planned it to begin with.

"I just love this place," she said, staring down at her menu as if it were a grandiose valentine. "Daddy always brought us here on Friday afternoons. That was when he was happiest, after work had let out for the week. One time he even let us order our desserts first. I remember Howard ate a banana split as long as this table." She looked up at Eastman and blushed. "I think he threw up afterwards."

Eastman could almost taste the marshmallow cream mixed with bile coming up into his own mouth, and for a moment felt something like compassion for her brother, for the whole fucked-up scenario, for the world that table-length banana splits had spawned. The music leaking out of the perforated circle of tin above their heads was of the same emetic vintage as everything else in Antoinette's: a gruff-voiced singer was emoting to his phantom lover in a slow-moving ramble, and every time the lugubrious chorus, "I'm your puppet," came around again, Eastman saw the same three homosexual black men, who, in the fifties when the song was recorded, had been shoved so far back in the closet, they had forgone their vocal chords and sung, as their one mocking protest, through their bound-up testicles. It was especially depressing to Eastman that anybody would want to hold on to such an era, though when he thought about it, about the shape things were in now, which was really no shape at all, he could at least grasp some inkling of it. People could say they'd *lived* during that time, which was more than they could say about what came after; it may have been awful, but at least they knew what it was.

Eastman suddenly felt as if he'd had too much to drink. "Maybe we could share something," he told Violet, who seemed caught in her nostalgic pose. "Maybe a nice big salad."

She looked up from her menu almost sleepy-eyed, as if she'd been wakened from a sweet and tenacious dream. "That's what Moonier always ordered," she said, quickly at attention again. "Salad was his favorite food, he told me once, even before he got sick."

"What was wrong with him?"

"Sadness," she said, as though repeating the very diagnosis of the specialist who had ferreted it from the endless list of things that could conceivably go wrong. "The cancer came along later, of course. But it was sadness that got the whole thing started. Moonier couldn't bear living in this world, even with me in it. He was born and raised a Mennonite, you know."

Eastman wasn't exactly sure who the Mennonites were, though he had it in his head they were clean-living pacifists who quietly disavowed the modern world while any number of its snipers casually took aim at them. "Is that why your brother didn't like him?"

"Partly, I think. And partly that Moonier was a good bit older than I was—he was forty-six when he died. Mostly Howard didn't like him because *I* did. Howard's the orneriest person I've ever met. Mama said 'no' was the first word to come out of his mouth. I think 'way' must've been the second."

Au contraire, Eastman thought: 'fucking' was the second word, 'way' was the *third*.

"We met right here in Antoinette's, though he'd quit his job as fry cook by then. We were only together nine months, eight of which we were married." She looked up suddenly at Eastman as though she suddenly understood that he'd been judging her. "Moonier knew what he wanted, and what he didn't want he took in stride—that was his strongest character. When the doctors told him he was finished, he just shrugged. He never went through them other stages."

"I thought you said he was sad."

"I said it was sadness that killed him." She looked incredulously at Eastman for a moment, the way the egg woman had when he'd asked her about Earthling, then let her eyes relax into her face again. "Moonier used to say the world was filled with so many sorrowful things, you could barely slip a straw through anyplace to do your breathing. Sadness he took for granted. That still don't mean it didn't smother him."

Eastman wanted to ask her why she would have married such a person, but he decided he might just as well ask why she dressed the way she dressed or talked the way she talked, or, really, why, as Chance had phrased it, she was so much the way she was. It was enough that she held the secret thing that kept people going, even if, in her case, that thing was composing elegies for people who had somehow lost it, people like her Mennonite husband and the scores of others who had slipped, without much commotion, from the face of the distracted earth.

A waitress wearing a hennaed beehive completed their semicircle of booth with her massive form. "Have you decided?" she asked, withdrawing a pad from her apron.

"On what?" Violet said. She had on the same straight face she'd used to sing her music.

"I guess you haven't," the waitress replied and stuck her pad back in her apron.

"We want a salad," Eastman said.

Violet laughed. "Oh, that. We'd like a number fourteen with Thousand Island. And could you bring the dressing on the side?"

"Just one?" the waitress asked, and when Violet nodded, the waitress returned the appropriate snide look and barged into the farthest depths of the restaurant.

Eastman was just remembering that he despised Thousand Island dressing when he saw the egg woman materialize from the bathroom, though she didn't seem to see him. Her walking, as it turned out, was even more labored than her breathing—the whole of her weight seemed to shift to whatever foot she was placing in front of her—though considering the awkwardness of her stride, she lumbered out of Eastman's view rather quickly, so that he had to shift his own body weight around to see where she would set down. He must have audibly gaped when she wedged herself into the booth next to the Asian man in the corner, because Violet, without seeing Eastman's face, asked, "What's the matter?"

"I thought I recognized somebody," Eastman said, turning back, just as their waitress sunk a tubful of iceberg lettuce layered with boiled-egg halves and orange-ripe tomato wedges, followed quickly by a gravy boat filled with mayonnaise and ketchup— the two seemed to have willfully segregated—onto the Formica table. A little jar of sweet pickle relish came with it, on the side.

"Well did you?" Violet asked.

Without answering, Eastman again shifted his attention to the egg woman, who seemed to be on familiar terms with this Asian guy, whoever he was. She even seemed to be showing him some respect, or her version of respect, which was to occasionally look in his direction when he was speaking to her. The Asian, on the other hand, maintained his aloof surveillance of the place without once, during

Eastman's brief observation, meeting the egg woman's eyes with his own.

"She didn't recognize me," Eastman said. "That's what really counts."

"For what?"

"It's just poker, that's all."

"I was never very good at cards," she said, as if admitting something of great consequence, and when he offered no more explanation, she seemed ready to launch into another of her nostalgic raps as a way of making him talk.

"She lives at the motel I'm staying at," he said. "In the room next door. Every morning I wake up to the advice she yells at herself."

"Is it very good advice?"

"If you believe in the power of clichés."

"I believe in the power of miracles," she said. "Though I can't say I've actually witnessed any yet myself. That's where beliefs come from, don't you think? From what we hope is true, not what we know not to be."

"I haven't given it much thought."

"You should," she said, and, bypassing a pair of

plastic scissor tongs that were propped up in the salad bowl, piled her plate full of lettuce using her bare hands. "I hope you like Thousand Island."

He watched her dump the relish into the gravy boat and churn it briskly, the way his sister stirred her iced tea, and then pour a thick layer of it over her salad.

"I played up there once, at Thousand Islands," she said. "It's one of the prettiest places I've ever been to. That's why I always order their dressing. We should never forget the pretty things in life, they're so few and far between."

As usual, Eastman couldn't tell if Violet was being intentionally maudlin, but he wasn't about to ask her; he was content at this point to eat his salad, and so apparently was she, because she didn't say anything else until the check came, which she insisted on paying. But she didn't have enough money to cover it, so Eastman had to make up the difference, a sum that turned out to be quite a bit more than his share.

As they got up to leave, he noticed that the egg woman and her mentor seemed to be stuck in the same bored position, as if they'd been asked to replay this scene a hundred times from the top without once being allowed to finish it. He wished he could be sitting at their table when all of the posturing came to an end, when the currency of their base commerce actually changed hands, but he decided there was an inverse relationship between legitimacy and the amount of time it took to close a deal, and from what he'd sniffed so far of the egg woman's business, they could easily be sitting there for hours before anything transpired.

Violet stayed inside herself all the way back to the motel, and once she'd parked in the courtyard and Eastman had extricated himself from Chance's Cadillac, he sat looking in at her behind the wheel, as though, in her smallness, she were a child lost in a pretend game of driving.

Finally, he asked, "Aren't you going to come out?"

"I don't think so, Frank."

"Well, I guess it's goodbye, then."

"I don't believe in goodbyes."

"I forgot," he said. "You only believe in miracles."

"I believe in you, Frank."

"Why? Because I'm here talking to you right now? Because when my lips move you hear a voice inside your head? A squirrel has as much faith in walnuts. Only I wouldn't call it faith."

She turned the key in the ignition, and the engine roared against the walls of the courtyard. "I know you're going to make it, Frank. I know it, even if you can't see it right now yourself." She reached out to touch his hand, which was holding onto her door, but he pulled it away and wheeled backward until he was resting at the lip of the swimming pool, several yards removed from Chance's car.

"And if I don't make it," he shouted, "you can write a fucking song all about me."

He started to laugh then, a high unbridled laugh, like the one, perhaps, of a death-row inmate, who, on the day of his pardon, is told he has an incurable illness. "Good luck, your sporeness," he blurted out. "I hope the wind blows you in your favorite direction."

She looked at him one last time—almost with embarrassment, he decided, though he wasn't sure if it was for him or for herself—and then backed the car out of the courtyard, bottoming out on the steep part of the driveway where it connected to the boulevard. An old Ford Fairlane, what in an earlier decade would have been an undercover police car, came up swiftly behind her, flashing its brights, and Eastman could see a large Hispanic family slumped together inside of it, their tired eyes looking as if they'd been adrift for days and were searching now, in the half-night of Anaheim, for a decent place to land. Violet didn't seem to notice them as she slowly straightened out her wheels, though when she finally started the Cadillac moving forward, their car followed at a respectable distance, as if they expected Violet, in her unsinkable deliberateness, to lead them to more hospitable ground.

On the way back to his room, Eastman saw, floating like an apparition behind the Snow White drapes, the rectangular glow of the egg woman's television. Maybe she had someone staying with her after all, he thought. He was about to knock on her door to see who might answer, but then decided he was in no mood to deal with the sort of person who would willingly cohabit with the egg woman, so he kept right on to the predictable emptiness of his own room, which lay just a few feet ahead.

When he tried opening his door, he felt resistance on the other side, and, after giving a fairly good push, saw it was his suitcase, lying open on the carpet, that was causing all the friction. He wheeled over the aluminum threshold and groped for the light switch, flicking it on, and for a brief moment was seized with horror as he met the vitreous eyes, composed mostly of pupil, that stared from the oddly serene face of Earthling—he was standing near the telephone as he ate french fries, one by one, out of the box left over from McDonald's.

Then a strange calm surged into Eastman himself—it wasn't that he felt any less imperiled, it was really more the opposite feeling: suddenly he understood that he was in the presence of his animal superior, and like a cornered rabbit who stoically gives himself to a fox, he sat motionless in his wheelchair, his entire body now paralyzed by a kind of evolutionary grace.

Earthling let the french-fry box drop onto the carpet and stood his ground until he was finished chewing. Then he went into the bathroom and returned with a glass of water, which he set on the nightstand, before setting himself onto Eastman's bed. The gesture seemed implacably human, and without realizing it, Eastman swiftly reentered the much grayer environment of human negotiation, to which he was more accustomed.

"I'm glad you've made yourself at home," he said.

Earthling picked up the glass of water and seemed to pour it directly into his stomach without swallowing. His pupils hadn't gotten any smaller, even though they'd been exposed to the light for a good five minutes now. "I live under a bridge," he said in a rapid and percussive voice, as though his words were being typed instead of spoken.

Like the troll that you are, Eastman thought.

"But I'm going to Thailand soon."

"Why Thailand?"

Earthling simpered and lifted one of his dirty bare feet, scanning its calloused undersurface before setting it on his knee. Then he looked directly at Eastman with an accusatory stare. "I'm not going there to whore."

"Nobody said you were."

This response seemed to satisfy Earthling, at least for the time being. The shiny blankness returned to his eyes, and he pushed his foot off his knee as though it weren't attached to the rest of his body. "The Japs will lay out three bills for a virgin," he said emphatically, though his voice, which was still coming out in bursts, was directed at the carpet. "They don't even dick with the brokers, just go straight to the father out in the fucking paddies. Then they do her right there on the golf course. Right on the fucking *green* if they've all putted out." He was shaking his head now, though he seemed to be performing out of rote instead of conviction, as if he'd adopted it from the egg woman as a way to expand his limited emotional repertoire. "After they zip up, they make her caddie the rest of the fucking round. With the Japs it's always the same: two birds, one stone."

He stopped here and looked at Eastman, and for a moment seemed as if he were thinking, though Eastman ultimately decided that he was merely experiencing a break in his own personal service. "I don't need a virgin," he continued, addressing himself once more to the carpet. "It don't even have to be a chick. Release is release, man—it don't matter where it comes from. I'm there to surf, not to whore. But I hear the break's good down in Bali, down at the fucking point, and you need a little piece to keep your luck burning out there. In that part of the world it ain't hard to wake up to a blow job."

He looked up suddenly as if Eastman had just voiced some quibble over his facts. "I tell you, Shirley, it beats the fuck out of a fucking clock radio. Sometime you ought to try readin the leaves with some little Thai mouth around your dick. You'll know which way the wind is blowin."

Eastman had an incredible urge to change the subject, but he sensed from Earthling's tone that he wouldn't be amenable to it. He was looking at his feet now, turning them and lifting them off the ground as if they were a pair of shoes he were trying on, which, if he didn't like, he could exchange for a different style. At some point—whether it was a sign from within or without, Eastman was unable to determine—Earthling became convinced they were the right feet after all; he set them neatly together, like a private coming to attention, then lifted his head to look, in his vacuous way, at Eastman.

"Beatrice can have her fucking tickets," he said. "You never get to Bali with that shit. Sooner or later you always wash up here." He looked for a moment at his feet again and then back at Eastman. "I'm takin the boat *outside* on this one. Beatrice don't know shit about travel. Never fucking leaves her room except to see the fucking Emperor. Rest of the time she watches game shows with that little shitass Maury." He was shaking his head again, only this time in a haphazard fashion, as if he were trying to dislodge an orbiting fly from it. "Fucking Maury, man. He won't know where to squat his narrow ass when they doze this place under. Beatrice—shit—she's a whole different story. Disney's gonna stick one of their fucking motors into her. She'll be handin out her poison apples on the fucking Snow White ride. But where does that leave Maury, man? They sure as shit won't be puttin Maury into one of *their* fucking cartoons."

For a change, Earthling's eyes had something behind them—the look was somewhere between disgust and desperation—and Eastman nodded as though he understood. He saw now that he had mistaken blankness for what was really a haystack of emotion: Earthling's eyes were a reservoir for everything he had ever felt, the way that black was an absorption of every color in the spectrum, and it was only by accident that some artifact of his lucid past would buoy to the surface still in one piece, like a fortune in an eight ball, with as little bearing on the practices of the ongoing world. It occurred to Eastman that Earthling had been doing some small variation of this same scene for so long now that whatever came out of his mouth was likely to fit in someplace, or even if it didn't, there was no one sane enough in his midst to tell him that what he was saying was inappropriate. His peers had long ago stopped putting meaning to his words, anyway, just as he had long ago stopped trying to generate it.

"You ain't got much shit here," Earthling said, looking downward at the suitcase. "Nobody carries valuables no more. Maybe they ain't got no more valuables to carry."

Eastman looked at the suitcase now himself, and they both watched it for a moment as if it might have something to say about this sorry state of affairs. His things seemed to have been gone through, though not in a hysterical or arbitrary manner: every sock, every shirt, every pair of underwear looked as if it had been inspected for clues to Earthling's own peculiar condition. Eastman could see now that he had gained access through the bathroom window, though somehow without breaking the glass; clearly he was a master at slipping into others' lives unnoticed, Eastman concluded, which was probably because he didn't recognize the boundaries between himself and the rest of the world. Breaking and entering—or really, Eastman thought, just the entering—had become second nature to Earthling by now; he wondered if the egg woman had enlisted this Maury as a defense against Earthling's encroachments.

"I carry traveler's checks," Eastman said, almost as an afterthought, and felt for his wallet in his pants—it didn't seem to be there anymore.

"Traveler's checks," Earthling repeated, as though he were helping Eastman with an inventory of his belongings. "You might as well sign them over to Beatrice right now. But Beatrice don't take checks. Beatrice has a strong preference for cash."

For a second a smile flickered across Earthling's face, an insider's smile, and Eastman looked back over his shoulder to remind himself that the doorway behind him really was still open. He wondered if Earthling had somehow gotten his hands on his wallet and remembered that they'd remained physically apart the whole time they'd been talking.

"So you're a cripple," Earthling said. "You a veteran?"

"Of sorts."

"Then you've seen Asia?"

"Not yet."

Earthling started to nod, though he seemed to stall again for a moment at the low point before his eyes retook their brittle varnish and his head came springing back up. "So you never went," Earthling said. "You and fucking Beatrice. She's a veteran, too. Of this fucking place. Tell me something, Shirley—how far down before it stops?"

"What do you mean?"

"Is it, like, at your belly button or your dick? Or maybe its a hair on the dimpled part of your ass?"

At this point Eastman considered excusing himself, but then he remembered that Earthling was in *his* room and not the other way around. He had no idea what Earthling was talking about, and he had no desire whatsoever to find out—just knowing might release the sort of panic-scented hormone Earthling seemed to be rooting around for.

"You have good pores," Earthling said matter-of-factly, though he was closely watching the movement of Eastman's eyes. "Mr. Jimmy used to tell me that and I didn't even fucking know what he meant." He laughed then, but it could have been another sentence, the sound of it was no more expulsive than his speech. "I could do you and you wouldn't even fucking feel it. That's what it comes down to, ain't it, Shirley?"

"But I'd know it," Eastman said quickly, though without lifting his voice. Then he was in his passive mode again, waiting for Earthling to perform his offhanded pounce.

Instead Earthling took a long breath and let his face go limp, then lay back on Eastman's bed with his arms at his sides. "What are you fucking doin here, man?" he asked, and his tone, instead of sounding territorial, struck Eastman as genuinely inquisitive, as if he were really asking, Why would anyone willfully put himself into such a situation? It was the sort of question that Margaret or his parents would have asked, and when he saw them sitting together in his living room back home, their faces set in the same solemn smile, he was all at once angry at Earthling for being in *his* room, for putting *him* on the spot, when all Earthling was was a fucking criminal, a fucking dead end on this fucking dead-end branch of half-baked Darwinism.

Eastman was about to tell him to get the hell out, when, without saying anything, Earthling hastily rose off the bed and disappeared out the bathroom window, as if, along with his other peculiar talents, he could read people's minds—though, likewise, Eastman thought, without any profitable end.

"I thought you might need this," he heard Violet's voice say, and when after a small struggle he had managed to get his wheelchair turned around in the cramped space of his room, he still thought she'd meant a hug, instead of his wallet, which rested like a piece of toast on her outstretched palm.

His dreams this night were filled with Earthling; he woke up so many times to an empty room that after a while he stopped trying to defend himself, even in his sleep. Earthling moved in and out of Eastman's body like a virus, invisible and ubiquitous and freely partaking of his soul. He had never been so thoroughly violated in or out of consciousness, and when the sun rose at last and he opened his eyes to the largest rat he had ever seen, he wasn't even scared—he was just so relieved that it wasn't Earthling.

The rat, which was the size of a small dog and the gray-brown color of a raccoon, had its back to Eastman, its naked, reptilian tail held in a loose coil around one of his socks. It was trying to force its head inside the french-fry box without much success, though Eastman doubted that Earthling would have left behind any crumbs anyway. Then the rat suddenly seemed to sense it was being watched; it turned its funnel-shaped head toward Eastman and studied him disinterestedly while Eastman yelled and waved his hands at it, to no visible effect. The thought then occurred to him that he was viewing some sort of zoological hoax, the creature before him was such a strange amalgam of parts.

"That's because you're not a rat," he said out loud, to what he now realized was an opossum, then watched as the thing casually retreated out the bathroom window, where, Eastman surmised, it would shortly join its brethren in the palm trees.

In the next room he could hear a television quietly playing and pictured a jockey-size Maury sitting in little Jockey shorts on the foot of his bed, his depleted insomniac's eyes staring dutifully into the screen while the egg woman slept loudly behind him. Eastman found this image oddly soothing and fell this time into a tranquil sleep and didn't wake up until well past noon, to what he thought was someone knocking—actually, it sounded more like pecking—on his door.

"Who is it?" Eastman asked, turning over onto his back, though he really didn't expect an answer.

"Sheets," he heard the Persian girl tell him from behind the wooden curtain of his door, and then listened to her footsteps disappear into the deadening sunlight. Not long after, he wedged his chair in the doorway and looked on the ground for the sheets, but he couldn't find them. Then he noticed the egg woman sitting in her usual position on the milk crate—the sheets, still folded, were draped like a huge napkin across the vast slope of her body.

"Saw you with your squirrelfriend last night," she said rather tepidly, as though she still had the ability to feel hurt about something. "She looked real familiar to me. Maybe we done business in the past. You should've reacquainted us."

"Violet travels just fine on her own," Eastman said, and with deliberate mystery added, "or at least with the help of Chance."

"My way leaves nothing to chance. You get what you want a lot quicker that way, don't you think?"

"I try not to think anymore. I try not to *do* anything anymore. Any effort on my part would just be wasted motion."

"A frigging philosopher. You wanna stop thinking? Look at Earthling—he couldn't think if he held a brain in each hand."

"That's some testimonial."

"Whatever you say, baby. The customer is always right. You wanna fry, I got somethin for you. You just wanna catch a few rays, I got somethin for you, too."

"What if I want to stay peaked? What if I want to stay in my room until I shrivel up and die?"

She made the parrot noise again. "Your peaked ass is halfway out your room already. Believe me, baby, your action is blaring right now. I can barely hear myself talk."

Eastman conjured up a sneer. "I don't see you taking any trips," he said. "Except to see the fucking Emperor."

The egg woman swallowed a sizable amount of air and then let it out slowly as if she were exhaling the smoke from an expensive cigarette. "Baby," she said, and it sounded almost like a term of endearment, "I took my last trip a long time ago. The plane crashed right where I'm sitting. It won't be flyin again anytime soon."

Eastman waited for more, but there wasn't any, and for the first time he realized that he had given the egg woman pause—though that was all it was; there wasn't any facial expression to reveal what she was thinking in the interim.

"Yeah, maybe I ought to send you up to see old Jarvis," she said presently. "He's like a principal for grown-ups, that Jarvis. He's like a school all by his-self. If you can't make up your mind, Jarvis'll frig-ging make it up for you."

She ferreted a hand into the breast pocket of her jump suit, withdrawing a pen and a waitress-size pad with a rubber band around it and began writing something on the exposed page. Eastman assumed that this Jarvis and the Emperor were the same person, though he wasn't about to ask, espe-cially since this was the first time he had managed to crack, for one moment at least, the egg woman's rubbery shell.

"You'll find the palace here," she said, and tore out the page on which she'd been writing, letting it dangle from the leftmost of her pudgy white hands. "You won't have any trouble with the guard. Just tell him Beatrice pointed you."

Eastman took the directions from her without studying their contents and shoved them into his shirt pocket. The egg woman rolled her goggles up onto her forehead so that they were reflecting the sky back to itself. "You got enough gas in that thing for a road trip?"

"I get good mileage," Eastman said.

"Take your sheets with you, baby. You may need a nap along the way."

She held them out from her in the same manner she had the directions, but for a change Eastman left *her* dangling, instead of the other way around. As far as he was concerned, she could hold onto them until he got back, if he ever got back, from this weird-ass journey, this boat outside, that she was sending him on now. Who knew what fabulous creatures he might meet along the way? He may not even *want* to come back to the Tradewinds, assuming he would have a choice.

The day was colorless and of a uniform glare, and the harsh light, instead of shining from the sun, seemed to project upward from some mysterious source on earth and lie flat against the sky. There was heat rising everywhere from the concrete in its various forms, from the benches and the streetlamps, from the structures holding parked cars and the structures built around the moving ones: the overpasses and underpasses, the freeways and driveways, the alleys and side streets and avenues—and the sidewalks, the raised and paneled concrete network along which Eastman, in his hand-powered wheelchair, was making his stunted progress.

After his accident, Margaret had insisted he buy an electric model, this battery-operated contraption with a joy stick for a throttle, but he told her he didn't need any fucking golf cart and the subject was never raised again. Yet her message had penetrated him thoroughly; as far as Eastman was concerned, she had really been advising him to abandon his own spirit—*Look where your energy has taken you now; you're lucky to still be alive!*—and he couldn't help but resent her after that, even though he was sure she hadn't consciously known what she was doing.

But it occurred to him now that she had been right; he could only write off so much of his predicament to happenstance, and look where his energy *had* taken him: he was panting and sweating and feeling as though he might pass out from heatstroke, while every block in this fucking kingdom looked practically the same—you couldn't even fucking tell what season it was. He felt suddenly like some wigged-out character in a low-budget cartoon, his wheels literally spinning as the cartoon backdrop kept looping behind him. But then he remembered you couldn't feel like that, you couldn't have an anvil drive you into the pavement and then crawl back out wearing a Band-Aid and a halo of spinning stars—that was the whole fucking point. The pain in this place was real; it was the pleasure that came at you in little white puffs of smoke.

Still there was no way he could rest—the egg woman with her baited mouth had made sure of that. He knew if he passed out he'd just be a Dorothy—the flying monkeys in this place would carry him away—and if a heart attack was in the cards, then so fucking be it. He could eat up a shit-load of profits in an ICU while the enabled ran their enabled routes and feigned sadness when they finally unplugged him.

The stoplight above the huge intersection ahead of him wasn't showing any colors yet—he recognized it as one of these new type the enabled were installing everywhere; they never wanted you to have too much information at any one time—it was all a part of their subconscious plan to obscure the big picture. He was relieved, though, to see that they hadn't yet altered the pedestrian signs: the pure bold letters of WALK silently taunted him for a few seconds before abruptly changing to their flashing red opposite.

"Thank God," he said out loud, and gave himself a couple of good thrusts so he could coast up to the curb and the crosswalk beyond it, though he wound up falling quite a bit short of his mark. The sequence of lights, that was part of it, too, he thought gratefully. Sometimes you could catch a break with a sheer roll of the dice. Or maybe they were part of the whole ingenious cruelty of the thing after all—you couldn't give out before they were done extracting your last few drops of blood.

He stared into the viscous lines of traffic while he tried to catch his breath, his head throbbing as if someone were halfheartedly strangling him. Then he realized he was seeing the first stirrings of rush hour, though he saw, too, by a large digital clock over what looked like a nearly defunct savings and loan—the clock seemed to be ticking off the draining millions as well as the minutes—that the time was just a little past three.

"Hey, Preence," a woman's voice said, in an exaggerated Mexican accent. "Djew gotta light?"

He tiredly swung his chair around and was surprised to find no one, outside of the unremitting swell of commuters, in his immediate vicinity. Then he spotted a woman several yards away near the entrance of an alley that ran between a strip mall and a huge apartment building that Eastman thought resembled a hospital. The woman was slowly wagging her finger—she seemed to have a whole array of exaggerated gestures—for him to come to her. "What's a matter, Preence?" she asked him. "Djew got bad ears, too?"

Her voice the second time around had the same intimate effect, even though, Eastman now realized, she was virtually shouting over the traffic; it was the best stage whisper he had ever experienced. He kept his eyes on her as he wheeled to where she stood, up against a cinderblock wall next to a dumpster that was painted a light gray, both of which blended perfectly with the concrete pavement and the white stuccoed back of the mall. He had never before seen an alley this clean or thematic, and when he got up close enough to get a good look at her, he realized she belonged to this place too, or, really, was a complement to it: she was dark-skinned, with short dark hair held back by an ivory band that had a little ivory bow at its crest, and beneath this was an open, small-featured face that had some quality that induced Eastman to smile. Maybe, he thought, it was the Heidi outfit she was wearing, this navy blue corset that was laced tightly over a flowing white peasant dress, complete with puffy white sleeves. Or maybe it was the odd way the shadowed late-afternoon light had of heightening her extravagant markings—she seemed almost to be superimposed on the hardscape; he couldn't imagine her arriving or departing there.

He blanched for a moment when he realized he was staring at her, then feebly patted his shirt pocket. "Sorry," he said, his breath now returned to him, "I don't have any matches."

She smiled briefly, though with a detectable amount of aggravation, and it occurred to Eastman that she wasn't holding a cigarette, nor was there anything flammable in sight—unless, he thought, she wanted to set herself on fire.

"You in a hurry?" she asked, all traces of her accent suddenly evaporated; her voice at this distance was like braille. "Because if you're in a hurry—"

She broke off her own sentence and turned her head sideways to look down the long empty shaft of the alley. Eastman followed suit, but he didn't see anything except a baggily clad teenager on a skateboard who flickered past them at the other end. When he looked back, the woman was staring at him with fixed and impatient eyes. She *wanted* him to be in a hurry, he understood now, and not the other way around.

In the meantime, she had repositioned herself against the wall, her dress parted on either side of a long, well-toned leg, all the way up to its gartered thigh. The dress wasn't so much slit as it was torn, though in a deliberate manner—it had become fashionable, Eastman remembered, to skillfully damage your own clothing and then appear without the means or inclination to repair it. Then he noticed a small tatoo curving around the inside of her thigh—it was the picture of a bearded gnome-like man showing off a gigantic erection. Beneath it, in little cartoon letters, it said HUMPY.

"Tick, tick, tick," the woman said, and abruptly redraped the leg. With embarrassment, Eastman lifted his head, understanding suddenly that he'd just been shown the wares by a prostitute version of Snow White. The hasty smile had returned to her mouth, an orifice which seemed to activate only after his eyes had lingered on it for a second or two: "You wanna look, it's the same charge you wanna touch. A bob—either one of us—is fifty. I never swallow. You wanna swallow, its your own business. The Act is a bill, and you got to use my condom. Like I said, if you'd rather beat off, it's the same price. Either way, it's ten minutes on the clock."

Her head nodded vaguely in the direction of the savings and loan, and Eastman imagined her announcing "Time's up" to some kneeling and hapless john who was hopelessly trying to digest her. Then his eyes refocused on the mouth, which seemed to be waiting for his attention again before settling into a determined purse. "And, no," it said forcefully and, at the same time, indifferently, "I don't do no anal."

Eastman watched the mouth for a couple more seconds before figuring out it wouldn't be saying anything else. He wheeled backward a few paces until he could take in her entire image again—for all of the enthusiasm she was projecting, she might have been waiting at a car wash.

"I'm really not interested," he told her, and watched her empty face aggressively stave off a reaction. "But I would like to ask you a question."

She shrugged. "You wanna talk, pay a fucking telephone." The taut line of her mouth was already slackening, however, and by the time he'd blinked, her lips had pooled into a laconic grin. "You ever see one of them phone-job chicks?" she asked him, though she might just as well have been addressing the alley.

He stared at her blankly, waiting for her next piece of hardened rhetoric. When she didn't say anything, he understood he was expected to participate in this little knock-knock joke of hers. "I've never even talked to one," he said.

"It's like this, Prince," she told him, her mouth suddenly contracting again. "You'd rather jerk to Joan Rivers. Now, I don't got time to negotiate here. You ask anyone on the street, Mariela gives you more fuck for your buck."

He took the directions out of his pocket and flashed them to her, just to prove he had a more quotidian motive. "I'm looking for Citruswood Avenue. Is it very much farther?"

"You goin to the palace?" she asked in a split second of amazement, before his own look of amazement must have told her that she had guessed it right. "You shoulda said so to begin with." She picked up the hems of her dress and began walking almost splay-footed toward the opposite end of the alley. She was almost there when

she stopped and turned around, as if, by some professional sense, she knew that Eastman had been
watching her. "What part of *you* could be for sale?"
she asked him, and her voice had that familiar
quality again. "You peddling rides in your wheelchair?"

If it hadn't been for Snow White's confirma-
tion, Eastman would have thought this whole af-
fair was another of the egg woman's crude jokes,
her dispatching him on this interminable one-
item scavenger hunt; his destination, as it turned
out, didn't have any structures you could even
remotely call a palace. Just beyond him stood a
two-story medical plaza sheathed over with heavily-
tinted Plexiglas, which he figured had the most
potential for some sort of front. Maybe this Jarvis
was a dentist gone bad, he thought, the kind of guy
they loved to feature on the true-crime shows
Margaret always seemed to have on, the proverbial
pillar of the community who anybody with half a
brain would recognize as a sociopath, but whose

friends and neighbors, most of whom were also so-
ciopaths, would express shock, on camera, to the
long list of cruel deeds he had undertaken.

Without too much trouble, Eastman managed
to get himself up into the curbed-in planter of ivy
that abutted the building and put his face against
the glass, his hands cupped around his eyes. A
waspy young receptionist with her hair in a twist
was staring back at him, her eyes full of that weird
brand of loyalty he had encountered in other re-
ceptionists; people like her didn't have anything
going for them except for their looks and a clear
sense of boundaries, Eastman decided, though he
had begun to see that this was about all it took to
get by around here. He could tell from her
unswerving blandness that if he didn't remove
himself from the planter soon, she would, by one
of her few and effective instincts, tap out 911 on an
outside line.

He rolled himself back onto the sidewalk just
as the light across to a many-acred strawberry and
mostly weed field turned green, and, with his mo-
mentum carrying him in that direction anyway,

kept on propelling his chair until he'd reached the other side. He set his sights on a fruit stand that was up a good fifty feet of a gravel-and-dirt uphill, a surface on which he had trouble finding his traction, so by the time he'd crested it, he was altogether winded again. The fruit stand, behind which stood a sausage-shaped aluminum trailer that for some reason he associated with the fifties and UFO sightings, consisted of a red-and-white-striped plastic canopy, held up by four aluminum poles that cast a thin shade over a large card table laid out with strawberries boxed in various configurations. At first Eastman didn't notice anyone overseeing the fruit, though his eyes quickly found a stoop-shouldered Mexican man, his slack face leathered by too many years in the unfiltered sun, sitting in a beach chair on the other side of the table. Eastman couldn't remember the last time he had physically looked down on anyone.

"Hello," Eastman said, and watched the old man nod almost imperceptibly, then saw a little green metal cash box sitting next to him in the dirt. The man laid one of his eroded hands over the top of it, and Eastman averted his eyes, looking now at the boxes of strawberries before him. They were separated into two camps: the strawberries on the left were large and firm and appeared uniformly ripe, while the strawberries on the right were much more irregular, both in size and color. Surprisingly, a single basket of the prettier strawberries was priced fifty cents less than a basket of the others. Eastman raised his head again, peering down at the old man, who seemed now to be on the edge of sleep or, for that matter, death—his eyes were just beginning to roll back in his head.

"Why are these more expensive?" Eastman asked him, raising a basket of the haphazard strawberries.

After a few seconds the old man, fully conscious again, lifted his hand from the cash box and sculpted it into a fist. A single finger rose slowly from the mass of flesh, while he held up his other hand, its five knobby fingers widely spread. "One fifty," he said with a heavy accent.

"Yes, I know that," Eastman said in an amplified voice, as though a higher volume could overcome a difference in language. "But why do they cost more than these others?"

"Because they taste like strawberries."

Eastman looked up and saw the young Asian man from Antoinette's standing at the entrance to the trailer. From the clear, elongated English that he spoke, Eastman pegged him as a native Californian, though he lacked the usual surfed-out drawl that crept from the mouths of the egg woman's clientele, a deficiency that Eastman realized was a manner all its own. He pitched his voice now with a quiet authority to the old man, though he spoke this time in a crisply worded Spanish. The old man, for his part, seemed to take his time absorbing what little meaning had been dispensed before lifting himself up from the chair and moving stiffly out of view, somewhere behind the trailer.

"It's a little bet we have," the young man said, stepping with a dancer's grace down the metal stairs and over to the table. He was dressed as sharply as he had been the day before, in undyed cotton twill pants and a rayon Hawaiian shirt that

featured silk-screened blue squids, each of which
stared from its gelatinous body with one large disappointed eye. Eastman watched him with appre-
hension as he systematically picked through a flat
of the good-looking strawberries, extracting a particularly large and red example, which he offered
to Eastman. "No thank you," Eastman said, where-
upon the man bit off half of it, chewing precisely
for a few moments before spitting the pulp out on
the ground and then grinding it into the dirt with
his shoe as if it were a cigarette butt. "Sawdust," he
said evenly, then reached, with his eyes still on Eastman, for one of the less-appealing berries. "These
are my father's recipe," he said, and smiled, though
without conveying the slightest hint of joy. Eastman watched him place the whole strawberry, stem
and all, on the trough of his tongue as he might a
vitamin pill, then close his mouth and eyes and
chew a few seconds before swallowing, after which
he opened them again and picked the stem off his
tongue as if it were a piece of lint. He seemed to
have perfected a host of rituals by assignment,
Eastman thought, though it was hard to imagine

who would have wanted him to do so, and for what motive.

"Ain't nothin like the real thing, baby," he said dully. "They really are worth the extra fifty cents, but the customers think they look sick. I told Rosario, 'You have to spray them if you want to get anything for them.' The Ag Board finds one medfly in a trap out in San Dimas, they spray the whole damn county, but Rosario won't spray his own worm-eaten strawberries. My father taught him all he knows, and he wouldn't spray them either. My mother, she got cancer anyway, so what does it matter? We all get cancer sooner or later. I just hope they have better drugs by the time my turn comes around."

He gave Eastman a penetrating once-over, then brought his focus back to an apparently uninspiring middle distance—at least not inspiring enough to cause him to speak. He didn't appear any more defined at this close range than he had in the restaurant, except it was easier get a fix on his ancestry—Japanese—and his age, which Eastman guessed to be roughly his own.

"The others I have brought in from Mexico," the man started again suddenly, though without any seeable impetus. "I don't know what they do to them to make them look like that. They could shoot them full of silicone, for all I know. The point is they sell because they look the way people think strawberries should look, and the margin on them is good because the poor bastards that pick them live in tents and don't have health insurance and get twenty cents an hour. Rosario works this whole field by himself and it still costs a buck fifty to produce one of his baskets. And the funny thing is, most of the customers think the others are Rosario's. He doesn't know enough English to set them straight."

He suddenly looked into Eastman's eyes, catching him off guard, and then smiled the same joyless smile. "But then Rosario's what I call an old dog. He doesn't understand the concept of discretionary income."

With one quick motion, almost as if he were drawing a pistol, he dropped his hand down over the table of strawberries for Eastman to shake.

"Jarvis Tayama," he said, and Eastman obliged him, at least involuntarily, allowing his hand to be moved in a rubbery union. "And I presume you're Frank Eastman," to which Eastman nodded—he couldn't remember if he had actually told the egg woman his name—whereby his hand was summarily released.

Jarvis moved back a couple of paces from the table and into the diminished light of the sun; it was as if he thought his meticulous image would be better received from this setting. "I've heard a few things about you, Frank," he said, looking vaguely askance and, all at once, tired. "You are a man whose motives are unclear. Which I might find curious, if I were a curious man."

What sort of man are you, then, Eastman thought, and then, figuring he had nothing to lose, asked the question directly.

The small amount of expression that Jarvis wore on his face vanished entirely. He brushed off a spot on the steps and sat down on it, taking a loose cigarette from his shirt pocket and a single wooden match from his pants. He put the cigarette in his mouth and with one hand struck the match, cupped it from the breeze, and lit the cigarette, all in the same deft motion. Then he put the spent match back in his pocket and gazed off toward the medical plaza as if he were on a break of some kind. "I'm a businessman, Frank," he said at last. "I thought that much was obvious by now."

"I guess I meant more in the spiritual sense," Eastman said, noticing the sound of his own voice as if it were someone else's. He had never considered himself a person preoccupied with spiritual matters—in fact, he had no idea how he would have answered such a question.

Jarvis emitted a tightly furled gust of smoke from the corner of his mouth. "Ah yes, the philosophy. Beatrice mentioned something about that. It leads me to think you have too much time to think about all this, Frank." He made a vague gesture toward the world at large, a slight raising of his free hand that he might have used to make a bid at an auction. "The whole scheme falls apart if you think about it. That's why people get paid to keep the scheme running, so none of them will have time to ask questions. The ones that do think about it, the ones that can't help themselves—well, you're talking about my clients' customers, Frank. The wig jobs are in that same company, though they're just more advanced versions of the rest."

He inhaled deeply on his cigarette as if to color whatever he might say next with smoke. "But to answer your question," he said, exhaling at the same time, "I am a businessman, Frank. It really doesn't go any further than that."

"What sort of business are you in?"

"Now that's a trickier question, Frank. It's a question I wouldn't normally answer, only because I wouldn't have time to answer it, since I, for the moment at least, am not one of my clients' customers. But since it is my day off, and since you are new around here, and since at some point in the very near future I hope you'll become a member of our little family, I'll indulge you this one time as a courtesy."

"Don't do me any favors," Eastman said.

"I don't do favors," Jarvis said matter-of-factly, and drew in on his cigarette—though he let the smoke out again before he had very much chance to savor it. "You might say I'm a facilitator."

"A facilitator? Of what?"

"Fireworks, chicks, reptiles. A lot of controlled substance. The occasional purloined automobile. Any merchandise that can't be acquired by legitimate means."

"Like strawberries."

He shrugged. "It's a fact of life that in order to validate my existence here, I need to report a taxable income, Frank. At least until the park boundaries have extended this far."

"And then what?"

"The *coup de grâce*, naturally. Disney buys my crown jewel here for a very large sum of money. The rest I've already sold off to other parties."

"I didn't know Disney bought shares in the black market."

"Of course they don't, Frank. It's the real estate they'll be after, for their next set of storybook rides." For one instant he looked extremely pleased with this notion, and then his face reverted to its mannered nonchalance.

"Why are you telling me all this?"

"Because you asked?"

"I mean, how do you know I'm not a cop? How do you know I'm not wearing a wire?"

He laughed in such a way that his eyelids shut until his last little explosion of breath. "What are you, an Ironside? Ray Burr is dead, Frank. His heart froze up on him a while back—Peter Jennings sang it to me from his little square cage." He was shaking his head now in an amused nod, though as if he were reliving a funny moment that he'd experienced many years, not seconds, before.

"I still don't get it," Eastman said, and Jarvis reached, it seemed instinctively, for another match and cigarette and again executed his lighting ritual. "Who are these clients of yours?"

"Dealers of one kind or another. Anyone who trades in the aforementioned products."

"So then you're a wholesaler."

"Come now, Frank. Do I look like a person who takes unnecessary chances? The penalty for possessing illicit merchandise is much too high."

"Then what do you do for your clients?"

"Perhaps it's this concept of 'doing' that's hanging you up, Frank. I suppose what I 'do,' in some traditional sense, is grease the wheels of commerce, though to say that is to imply that I wear a set of coveralls and go about the neighborhood with an oiling can. Of course, there is no grease, and there are no wheels, though there most certainly is commerce, and yet even that term is so broad as to remain virtually meaningless. Or is it actually meaningless? Do you see what just happened here, Frank? Even the briefest mention of commerce invites one to misinterpret what it is." He paused to take another puff on his cigarette, and Eastman noticed that he was smiling: he seemed to have been listening to, even getting off on, the rhythm—or lack of one—in his own stilted speech.

"Are you saying you're a promoter?"

Jarvis vaguely shook his head. "If you think about it, Frank, which I am in no way advising that you should, promotion in this line of work is problematic at best—how, for instance, does one advertise a cut-rate rock of cocaine, or the aphrodisiac properties of a certain endangered lemur? The traditional media are clearly not an option. But there is a medium—which you must already have experienced, Frank, or you wouldn't be here right now—known commonly as 'the word on the street—' "

As if on cue, Jarvis lifted his head from his teacherlike reverie, just as the old man pulled up to them from around back of the trailer in a large white pickup truck whose perfect state of cleanliness caused Eastman to turn his head, it so ably reflected the now visible and bloated sun behind them. He heard a car door open, but he didn't hear it shut it again, and in another moment, Eastman watched as the old man's corrugated body dropped into the lawn chair on the other side of the table, his face still an open disavowal of emotion.

"It's time I took you home, Frank," Jarvis said, in a manner that precluded Eastman from arguing with him—none of what Jarvis said could be argued with, he thought, though he still wasn't sure why—and then he maneuvered around to the passenger side of the truck and hoisted himself in, after which Jarvis quickly folded up his wheelchair, lifted it into the bed of the truck, and neatly strapped his own lithe body in behind the wheel. The mirrors apparently had already been set for him, or he assumed that they had, because instead of checking their positions, he took the cigarette from his mouth and balanced it in the already pulled-out ashtray. Then he placed the truck in drive and without seeming to look, launched it into traffic using the same unchallenged authority that had so far guided the rest of his behavior.

At the first stoplight they hadn't yet resumed their question and answer, mostly because Eastman was still grappling with the few tangible facts Jarvis had managed to disseminate. But by the second stoplight Eastman clearly understood his lack of understanding: he still had no idea, in any real sense, of what Jarvis did for a living.

"So the word on the street is you're an emperor," Eastman said, and looked out his window—a small group of misshapen people stood waiting at a bus stop. "Maybe what you do is collect taxes."

Jarvis, who was driving very fast in the slow

lane, swerved left at the last possible second to avoid hitting a parked car. "Oh, Frank," he said, sounding genuinely disappointed, "I thought we'd moved beyond this thinking business." He picked up his cigarette, which was miraculously still burning, and took a long marijuana-size hit off it before setting it back in the ashtray. "Doesn't an emperor offer at least a few things to his subjects? His leadership, say, or his armies, or, for that matter, his edicts? I offer none of these things, Frank. I am not in a position of authority over anyone except Rosario. He is my sole employee."

"So why should anybody pay you, then, if there's no reward for paying you, and no penalty for not paying you?"

"You haven't been listening very carefully, Frank. I never said my clients weren't rewarded for paying me; I'm merely saying that from my point of view I don't give my clients anything worth paying for. As far as I've been able to determine, not that I'm in the process of actually determining anything, their actual—or is it virtual?—reward for paying me is the mere lack of, as you termed it, a penalty, though I'm certainly not the one to dispense that penalty or even authorize its execution. Then again, all of what I've been saying represents my point of view, Frank, and *my* viewpoint here is immaterial. What really counts is that my clients *believe* they're being rewarded by my service, such as it is, and thus are compelled to reward me in a manner in which I *believe*—I run a cash-only business, Frank. And I suppose that makes a convenient analogy; like the paper currency with which I'm paid, my service has little or no intrinsic value. What it does have, what any medium of exchange has, is the faith of the people who use it that it represents value. Faith, Frank. That's what this whole thing comes down to."

"But why should anyone have faith in you?"

"Don't you have faith in me, Frank?" he asked, with what Eastman construed as actual sincerity, and then suddenly he was pumping the brakes, bringing the truck to rest just short of the car in front of them, which unlike the cars traveling beside it, had stopped at the intersection before the light turned red.

"I can't say that I do."

"But you do, Frank. You have faith that I can deliver you safely to your motel."

"I'm not so sure about that."

"In other words, if you thought I was drunk or senile or legally blind, or had never driven a car before, or didn't know the area, you wouldn't have gotten in this truck with me. Just as you wouldn't have gotten in this truck if you'd met me in a context you weren't comfortable with—for example, if I'd been a stranger offering you a ride on some dark freeway shoulder. You see, Frank, the word on the street has already accrued to me some power that I wouldn't have without it. My calling card is sending out its little tap roots, Frank—they're just beginning to take hold of your consciousness."

For one short moment Eastman felt the cold reach of tendrils—the follicled ends of his own fine hair?—probing in through his skull; he sat up straight in his seat and looked over at Jarvis, whose hands were fit loosely over the wheel. His face as it looked out into traffic retained its cast of manicured disinterest, and Eastman realized that he truly didn't care whether he made himself understood or not.

"OK," Eastman said, trying hard not to sound flustered. "I have faith that you'll get me back to my motel. I believe you really can pull off this one small feat. But these other people—I don't understand—why do they *need* to have faith in you? Surely you don't offer them rides."

The light turned green and the truck eased, as if being towed, into the intersection, following close behind the car ahead of them. It was as though Jarvis was a passenger now himself, and for a second Eastman recognized on his face that look of horror-filled longing borne by riders on a roller coaster as they crest its first, steep incline toward their simulated doom.

"Human motivation," Jarvis said, and stared, as if through the obstacles all around them, to a much less cluttered horizon. "Now we move into the realm of high speculation, Frank. You do realize, don't you, that I'm about to sell you a portfolio of junk bonds?" But he didn't wait for a reply. "The word on the street, Frank. I listen to it all the time.

If I could get it on the radio, I would. If the word on the street says that something is so, then it is so, whether or not it defies what you might think is logical. Maybe it's that a lot of my clients are superstitious, Frank. They've arrived here through a series of personal miscalculations, many of which are too horrible to face, so they need to believe in charms, in symbols of luck, *good* luck, which is what they tell themselves they've lacked up to now.

"And then of course the question becomes, why should Jarvis Tayama, of all people, represent good luck to them? That really is a good question, Frank. Maybe it's some misguided racial stereotype they've put stock in: the inscrutable, cricket-wielding Eastern man who spouts cookie fortunes and kicks to death all the bad people. Then again it could very well be the opposite. It could be that I stand for nothing, that the very fact that I am *not* a police officer, or a parole officer, or a social worker, or a priest, that I'm none of the things they've lost faith in, that I have no *legitimate* claim on them— that I have no claim, period—is the very thing that gives them faith in me. Or it could be some combination of the two. Or it could be neither. It could be that I perform the role of silent therapist, that I'm an unwitting passer of nourishment, like a sparrow defecating dandelion seeds onto a vacant lot. Maybe they see me as their representative, Frank, their ambassador, their chamber of commerce. Maybe I'm a habit to them. Maybe I'm a trend. Maybe I'm a goddamn hula hoop.

"Or maybe, in their heart of hearts, even though their lives have turned to shit, they need to feel someone understands what's happening here. Maybe they think I can see the strings, Frank. Maybe some even think I'm the one that pulls them."

"I thought Disney had that job."

"Do you see what I'm getting at here, Frank? If you follow any trail long enough, it disintegrates. That's the only place thinking ever takes you. All I do is make contact with them in some public place, exchange a few words, and then, if all goes well, receive payment. I'm a fixture, Frank, a part of doing business in this neck of the woods, and I was a fixture long before any of this current batch ever got here. The word on the street is what I've been scanning my whole life, and now, through some process which of course I don't understand—I don't even try to understand—I've become a part of it. I've learned to live within its parameters, Frank, but its parameters are impossible to describe. What we're experiencing this very moment is a chaotic system, but it's still a system—the connections are there, they just don't happen to make any sense. Today a praying mantis in a Guatemalan rain forest sheds its skin, and tomorrow a bat-eared landlady in Niagara Falls snips her TV cable with a pair of gardening shears. You can stare at it for the rest of your life, Frank, and you still won't see anything. It just doesn't bear the weight of scrutiny."

Suddenly his eyes widened as though he were experiencing a spasm of some kind, and then he briskly rolled down his window, cupping a hand over his left ear. "Did you hear that, Frank?"

"Hear what?"

"Listen, there it is again."

Eastman sat forward in his seat and closed his

eyes, though all he could hear was the sound of air rushing inside the truck.

"Pay Jarvis five percent of gross receipts," Jarvis said in a quavery Boris Karloff voice, and then, laughing, rolled his window back up. "The word on the street, Frank. That's what it sounds like if you know how to listen."

"Har-dee-har-har," Eastman said and opened his eyes, just in time to see the huge black refrigerated semi traveling alongside them start to merge into their lane. Jarvis veered into the next lane to avoid a collision and came up on a florist's van that had braked for no apparent reason, which he avoided only by cutting off the honking driver in still the next lane over. The truck stopped just before striking—in fact, it may actually have grazed—a fiftyish man in Speedos, water dripping off his long, sculpted physique, who, inexplicably, had decided to streak across traffic. In horror, Eastman watched the man dash through the far right lane, a motorcycle skidding around him, and then negotiate a parking lot of broken asphalt before disappearing into an actual neighborhood, an early housing tract of tree-lined streets, without even once breaking his athletic stride. The only thing more amazing to Eastman was how quickly traffic resumed—it was as if the drivers had grown used to wayward pedestrians hurtling themselves indiscriminately into their paths—and it wasn't for another block that he had recovered sufficiently to proceed with his interrogation.

"You mentioned a penalty," Eastman said now, and looked over at Jarvis, who looked as he usually looked—as if he were faithfully carrying out some detailed and arbitrary plan. "What happens if one of your clients doesn't pay?"

"Then I will no longer provide my service to him," he said, and stifled a yawn with his fist. "He will have lost faith in the system, or have gained too much faith in his ability to exist outside the system, which boils down to the same thing. His customer base will slowly dwindle, along with his reserves. Eventually my remaining clients will recognize him as no longer one of their own, and the word on the street will be altered to reflect his newfound status."

"That's it? You mean this whole thing is about status?"

"If you're not a part of the system, you're a free agent, Frank, just like you are now. Free agents don't belong here—they don't belong anywhere—and when you don't belong in a place, bad things will tend to happen to you. Maybe first they'll take your wallet. That's pretty much the standard. Then it might be your watch. Sooner or later they'll get around to your clothes, then the rest of your personal belongings. Believe it or not, Frank, I know a pawnshop out on College that hocks wheelchairs. The owner shines them up and puts them in his window for all the legitimate world to see. Pawnshops are where it all comes together, Frank. That's where the black market fades into the gray."

"It sounds like you're making a threat to me."

"You really want to take this personally, don't you?" Jarvis took his eyes off the traffic a moment to look at Eastman—it was as if he were consulting a map—then stared blandly again through the windshield. "Up to now you've seemed like a reasonably intelligent person, Frank, but I'm beginning to wonder. Haven't you been checking this place out? There's nothing even remotely personal about it."

"And yet you're telling me that if I don't buy one of your products, or excuse me, one of your clients' products, a lot of bad things are about to happen to me. That doesn't sound like a threat to you?"

"Oh, it *is* a threat—make no mistake about that—it's just not personal. None of this has anything to do with what I want or don't want. At the moment I'm just the messenger, Frank. I'm merely rebroadcasting the signals that are already out there. Who knows where they originate? I only know how things work around here, not how they *should* work."

"But you could stop these people from harming me."

"How would I do that?"

"Tell them I've made a purchase."

"But you haven't, Frank. My saying that you have won't make it so." He was shaking his head again, only this time when he stopped, he looked for one brief moment as if he were intensely nauseated. "You're a strange cat, Frank. A curious, curious cat. You would have gotten along well with my father. He was always asking questions, just like you, though he tended not to ask them out loud quite so much. But he did have that same look on his face that you have: a little anger, a little confusion, a little 'Why me?'"

"Maybe because he had you for a son."

"Yes, I'm sure he would have much preferred you—though the paraplegia he wouldn't have cared for. But that's another story. Or maybe it's not. Either way, I'm in a quandary right now, Frank. Here you are bent on communication, and the traditional lines of communication have failed, as they inevitably do. I'm starting to think—and you know how that's against my better judgment, Frank—I'm starting to think that a fairy tale might be in order here, a little bedtime story, since our time together is drawing to a close. I don't guess the boys in Disney's legal department would mind very much in this one case, do you?"

Eastman looked at Jarvis and snickered and

then decided that he might really be serious after all. "Is it going to be more bullshit?" Eastman asked him. "Or does this story have a point?"

"It's just a story, Frank. You know, like 'Hansel and Gretel.' It has a point if you think it has a point."

"Why do I get the feeling you're going to tell it to me whether I want to hear it or not?"

Without signaling, Jarvis abruptly turned the corner onto another crowded boulevard, and they were quickly enveloped again, this time by a new wave of encapsulated drivers. "Once upon a time— that's how these things usually begin, Frank. Some might call it a cliché, but I prefer to think of it as a convention."

"Just get on with it."

"Once upon a time, in a beautiful and faraway land surrounded on all sides by the ocean—"

"You mean it was an island?"

"Yes, Frank," he said somewhat impatiently, "it was an island. Actually it was several islands. But they would definitely qualify as large islands. We're not talking about an archipelago here."

"Do they have a name?"

"Pardon me?"

"These islands, do they have a name?"

"Of course not, Frank. There are no place names in fairy tales. You know, for universal reasons."

"Of course not," Eastman said, and held his temples with his hand.

"If you would prefer, Frank, I can give them a name." Jarvis scratched his head disingenuously. "Let's say 'Eastland'?"

"So this Eastland is in the East?"

"Yes, Frank, Eastland is in the East. Anything else?"

"Not at the moment," Eastman said and began rolling his head along the axis of his neck.

"So as I was saying, on the southernmost island of *Eastland*, where the days were mild and the growing season long, there lived a family of peasant farmers: a man, a woman, and their two sons. Life had been good to this family so far, Frank—they had worked hard but been fairly compensated—and, besides, the town where they lived *was* beautiful. They were happy, that's the bottom line of it, and even if it was that boring pastoral kind of happiness, they didn't know any different, so what does it matter? Everything was cool, that's what I'm getting at here. In fact, a relative peace had ruled the land as a whole for centuries, owing mostly to its isolation.

"But change was definitely in the air, Frank, not so much from within, but from without. For it seems that a very strange and powerful land that lay far across the sea—*Westland* as you would have it—had dispatched its emissaries, aboard a fleet of strange and powerful ships bearing strange and powerful weapons, to the capital of Eastland for the purpose of establishing her as a trading partner. Now on the surface this may have seemed like a harmless, even laudable, gesture on the part of Westland, but Eastland knew better. For she had recently watched an ally of Westland's wreak havoc on one of Eastland's very large neighbors merely because she had declined to strike a deal similar to the one now being offered by Westland. Well, the deal wasn't a very good one for Eastland—she would be giving up much more than she would be receiving—but the handwriting was on the wall, Frank, and the pact was made, and soon a new emperor with a new if-you-can't-beat-em-join-em philosophy rose to power and immediately ordered that Eastland move from its relatively modest agrarian self to the strange and powerful ways of Westland as fast as she possibly could.

"Unfortunately this new edict didn't go over too well in Eastland. Many people, who had clearly understood their roles in the old system, suddenly found themselves no longer useful in the new one, though at the same time having to give up more and more of their shrinking paychecks to finance it, which of course they made quite a fuss about. But this new emperor ruled with a firm hand, Frank, and the changes went ahead as scheduled, though fortunately for our family, since they lived in a place of temperate climate where two crops could be grown a year instead of one, their contribution to the new system wasn't so difficult to manage. Their lives of bucolic splendor continued virtually unchanged."

"As in 'happily ever after'?"

Jarvis took another hit off his cigarette and stabbed it into the ashtray, which he then clapped shut. "That sort of thing comes at the end, Frank. When you're being told a story, you're supposed to listen, not ask questions."

With one hand he steered around a catering truck that had temporarily monopolized their horizon. "Well, as I've stated, so far our family has emerged from all of this turmoil relatively unscathed, but not for much longer. For one day a stranger comes to town—isn't that how it usually goes, Frank?—a stranger from that strange and powerful land that lay far across the—"

"Westland?"

"Yes, Westland. And this stranger brings with him an offer: any young man with skills in farming can earn untold riches on still another island, this one tropical, that lies far out to sea between their two fair lands—let's say *Midland*—which, by the way has also come under the recent and undue influence of Westland. At any rate, the deal this stranger makes is was what you'd have to call a sucker offer, Frank. But when you're eighteen and you still don't get that adventure is a euphemism for a lot of horrible bullshit, you just go for it, which is what our number-two son does. He says goodbye to his family, despite what they've told him about similar in-the-end sour deals, and sails to where the sugarcane grows tall, so beginning his new life as a glorified farmhand.

"And of course, as I've already implied, the luster wears off quickly. The hours are long and the conditions insufferable, but our protagonist has foolishly signed a long-term contract, and the plantation owners—you know how they are—aren't about to let him breach it. So by the end of his little stint in slavery, primitive emotions like pride, which he figured had left him forever, have begun to stir in him again—he can't go back home and save face, Frank, and yet he isn't about to stay on in the cane fields of Midland. Fortunately about this same time rumors begin circulating that work can be had in Westland, and since, according to these same rumors, real estate can also be purchased there, and since our protagonist has managed to save most of his wages, he figures, why not? So he sails again and he lands again and he farms again, and pretty soon he buys a little patch of prime dirt, which is all he can afford, but it is in a beautiful and temperate part of Westland, the far west of Westland, as a matter of fact, and soon after he meets a girl, just arrived from Eastland, and they do the courtship thing and the marriage thing and the family thing, and before he knows it, our protagonist is basically doing his Eastland shtick only he's in Westland. Everything is copacetic, Frank, or pretty much copacetic, considering he's gone through all of this to be where he'd be anyway, except that now the rest of his family is thousands of miles across the ocean and he has to put up with a whole lot of extra shit because most of the people in Westland, who themselves, by the way, have come to Westland from other lands, look this different way than the folks from Eastland—call it a quirk of nature, Frank—and they even have the nerve to lord it over the Eastlanders as though they had a choice in the matter. You know how that minority rap goes.

"Nevertheless, our protagonist slowly accumulates more and more land, and with it more and more wealth, and he's really starting to groove on this Westland trip, which is all about accumulation, at least of a material kind. And with his own son coming of age and following in his farming footsteps, he's happy to be in Westland, Frank. He finally feels like he's a part of it. He's on the inside now looking out.

"Then of course the weirdness strikes—you know about the weirdness, right, Frank?—well, in this case it goes like this: one day our protagonist is sitting on his porch staring out over his now vast holdings when he hears, via a strange and powerful device—the sort of device that's become a specialty of Westland—that Eastland, who by now has learned well the ways of Westland, has, in a kind of preemptive strike, made an attack against Westland's navy, which for expansionary reasons is anchored in, of all places, that island paradise of Midland. This occurrence naturally upsets our protagonist even if he does find it understandable; he is, after all, and has been for many years, a taxpaying citizen of Westland, and as such feels that an outrageous act like this one must not go unpunished. So it comes as an especially rude awakening when a short time later the government of Westland, after first declaring war against Eastland, next declares that all persons of Eastland ancestry must immediately sell off their assets, in less than a week's time, in order that they be concentrated in guarded camps scattered throughout landlocked areas of Westland. And naturally it follows that under these extreme conditions a buyer's market would come to full bloom, Frank, which is exactly what happens, and our protagonist, in the grasp of despair, liquidates his holdings for a small fraction of their actual worth, and in the next breath he and his family are whisked off to a camp faraway in a cold and desolate valley, where they live in shame for the next several years. Which is really quite tragic, Frank, because our protagonist never lives to see his freedom again. He dies in the camp a bitter and brokenhearted man."

Jarvis fell silent then, though Eastman didn't

perceive any look of closure on his face. It was as if he had never told a story at all.

"So that's it?" Eastman asked him.

"No, no," Jarvis said, as though remembering something he'd wanted desperately to say. "This is one of those generational tales, Frank. Where there is Frankenstein, there is son of Frankenstein, is there not? And so the son of our protagonist, who as I've said has only recently come of age, is determined, as an act of defiance against the grave injustices perpetrated against his family, to carry on his family's tradition, even if his father is dead and his mother is in rapid decline, and he still finds himself encamped in a fortress of barbed wire. Thus he goes about locating a suitable mate, which isn't too difficult considering the vast pool of captive females in his midst, and soon he meets a young woman, who like himself was born in Westland and who feels his same sense of abject betrayal, and together they plot their clouded future, holding desperately to their faith that they will one day be liberated and given a chance to prove themselves.

"And sure enough, in the days shortly following their marriage, this moment arrives, though as usual, it is of a deeply paradoxical nature. It seems that Westland, which has been winning its war with Eastland, has, as if overnight, developed a strange and powerful weapon based on the theories of a pacifist genius, which it detonates in the skies over the southernmost island of Eastland, over the very town, which is now actually an industrial center, where our protagonist was born and where his family still lives, or did live, before the ensuing fireball lays waste to everything. This weapon is so strange and so powerful, in fact, that Eastland is, figuratively speaking, brought to its knees—as it was so many years before at the hands of Westland—and with his roots to Eastland now literally eviscerated, the son of our protagonist and his new wife are transported back to the scene of his father's once vast holdings, where, penniless, they begin the cycle all over again.

"Well, ten years go by, Frank, and with it a good deal of sweat at low-paying jobs, and still our couple has managed to maintain their spirits and a modest savings account to boot, which they use to buy a small farm, and shortly thereafter, along with their first harvest, a child is born, an only son, and things are really beginning to look up, Frank. Our couple has finally put the past behind them and they've begun to view themselves as full-fledged Westlanders, which, of course they are, and the son of our protagonist even starts having the same dreams his father had—you know, that whole generational fantasy—and for the first time in their lives, as far ahead as they can see, there is nothing but blue sky.

"But guess what, Frank? Weirdness, the sequel. Only this time weirdness is much less sudden, much less tangible than a mere act of war, which makes it naturally all the weirder. It begins really with the erection of an amusement park, in the very neighborhood—if that's what you'd call grove upon grove of oranges—where our couple has taken up residence. But this isn't your typical amusement park, Frank. For starters, it takes up a hundred or so acres of prime farmland. Second, it's not really an amusement park at all: this park—and it's the first of its kind in the world, Frank—this park is what's called a theme park. Gone suddenly are the days of carnival as sexual metaphor, as haven of lust and nausea and vague feelings of doom—well, maybe I have to take back that one. In its place comes a land—it's not even called a park anymore—a virtual nation within a nation. But instead of borders being established by geographical boundaries such as rivers and oceans, this land, even though it does have a physical dimension, is more or less a concept, just as the land in which it's contained—Westland—is more or less a concept itself, a place, at least according to the ads, where people come to fulfill what they can't fulfill in their native lands, though exactly what is never made very clear.

"Now at this point you're probably wondering just what is the theme of this brave new land? And the answer as it turns out, paradoxically enough, is that it's the very same theme of Westland. And then you naturally might ask, Well, why would anyone pay to experience what he can have for free? And the answer in this case is to remember that the thing we're dealing with here is a theme, an assertion, as opposed to, say, an objective reality, which in Westland is oftentimes filled with these ambiguous, even horrific, moments that weren't included as a part of the package. But where Westland staggers miserably, this new land, in its themeyness, offers up life the way it's supposed to be, without any of the other crap, even if it is a façade, not the real thing at all, a fact which, strangely enough, it doesn't attempt to hide from any of its customers, who are more than willing to pay precisely because it's *not* the real thing, since real is not what it should be, according to the promise of Westland.

"Unfortunately for our couple, the subtlety of all this is lost on them; they're not sure quite what to make of this new monstrosity in their backyard, but they figure, in their jaded-but-simple-people-of-the-earth kind of way, that there's still plenty of arable land in the vicinity to expand their own operation, so this thematic land can't be all that bad—though, as usual, they've underestimated the strangeness and powerfulness of Westland. It so happens that the owner of this new land, himself a product of Westland, has access to an even stranger and more powerful device than the one that decimated our couple's ancestral hometown back in Eastland. For this device has been planted in the homes of people throughout the vast stretches of Westland, delivering images of his new land and its theme across known demographic borders and directly into the hearts and souls of the Westlanders who voluntarily watch this device, who, in fact, have willfully paid for this device with their own hard-earned money. The result is that people come streaming to the new land by the trainload and carload and whatever else kind of load, and there are so many of them that there isn't enough lodging within the new land's boundaries, so that new lodging and new restaurants and new shopping centers—whole new neighborhoods, in fact—start popping up on the land all around the new land. And it's really just a snowball effect, Frank, because these visitors like what they see here in this temperate and westernmost part of Westland, especially since back home the theme of Westland has already begun to wear off, and they figure they'll get a new start out West, the way their ancestors got a new start when they first came to Westland to begin with. So in a matter of years what was once a fertile farmland is now carved up with people and houses and businesses and schools and whatnot, and whatever problems the new people thought they'd left back home of course they've brought with them. Meanwhile, land prices have skyrocketed and our couple owns the only farm left for miles and miles, and their son, who has grown up in the broad shadow of this new land, even attended universities within that same shadow, doesn't give a damn about agriculture—he can see it's the way of the past, Frank—while the father, who, despite all the shit thrown down on him by Westland through the years, has nevertheless kept buying into the theme of Westland, at least the economic part of it, the part that says that if a person works hard he can get what he wants, when really the best he can get is what he can *have*, which in the end is a partitioning of everything that he wants.

"So in a sea of motels and hamburger joints, the father attempts to reconcile these last unreconcilable events. But he winds up blowing his brains out instead, with yet another strange and powerful device."

Jarvis suddenly pulled the truck up to the curb, and Eastman was surprised to see that they had already reached the stuccoed walls of the Tradewinds, which stood out like a movie-set fortress against the dark pink sky.

"The End," Jarvis said, with no more investment than he had anything else. Several cars had already stacked up behind them, honking their horns, though, as before, Jarvis merely went on with his business—which at this point seemed to be staring into the little cluster of palm trees in front of the building—despite a sign expressly ordering him not to stop between the hours of 3 and 6 P.M.

"That's not much of an ending," Eastman said.

"Oh yes, I forgot. You wanted it to have a point. The moral of the story is there is no moral, Frank. Now that you mention it, there really even isn't any story. Around here you're either in the market or you're on the market; that's the only thing you need to remember. Various forces will put you in one slot or the other. You can call them market forces if you want to, Frank. I'm sure you've heard of the Invisible Hand."

Jarvis extended his own hand, barely visible in the sepia twilight, which Eastman, out of reflex, took hold of.

"It's been nice chatting with you, Frank," Jarvis said. "My only advice is that you develop a vice quickly, or at least a more popular one. In the end, I'll profit more that way. Believe me, there's no future in this Grand Inquisitor trip. People get paid to answer questions, not to ask them. Your time would be better spent acquiring a guardian angel."

This time Eastman let go of Jarvis's hand first. "What if I told you I already have one?"

"And who might that be, Violet Slimp? She hasn't done a very good job for you up to now, Frank. She can barely take care of herself, if you haven't already noticed. Tell me something, is she still married to that Christian speed freak?" The dark shape of his head turned to face Eastman. "No, that's right," he said, as if for once he hadn't known where his own monologue was taking him. "Maybe she'll sing hymns at your funeral, too."

They sat together not saying anything in what was now essentially darkness, while the cars kept inching past them, some of whose drivers, Eastman sensed—he had his eyes closed now in a kind of meditation—were firing invective, at close range, into their cramped quarters. "You know I won't be able to get out here," Eastman said after a time. "I couldn't get out here even if I still had my legs."

"You should be staying somewhere else then," Jarvis said, and without turning on his headlights, drove the truck what little distance remained to the courtyard.

For quite a while after he'd been left off, Eastman sat in the wake of Jarvis's exhaust, staring into the thicket of cactus at the center of the pool. Eventually he convinced himself that he'd seen the little white cat stir deep within it, and then satisfied, began wheeling up to door number five, where he knew the egg woman would be waiting.

It was all a conspiracy, he understood that now, but it was only a conspiracy of weirdness: it wasn't that these people shared any plan per se, it was just that they smelled some peculiar something on each other, and they could resolve it from a distance of several miles. Still, it was a talent that Eastman knew he didn't possess—at this point the only thing he could smell was his own sour perspiration—and in the next moment he vowed to himself that he wouldn't try to read between the lines anymore, he would only make the decisions that were right there in front of him. It wouldn't matter if Walt Disney, newly thawed from his deathbed on ice, were the one presenting him with choices.

Even so, he was surprised, even disappointed, to see the egg woman sitting in her customary place, now amid a little zone of porchlight, with his sheets lying at its periphery, apparently where she had tossed them hours before. When he came into her field of vision, she looked acutely in his direction for a few seconds before her eyes receded, and her mouth, which had been poised to speak, quickly softened into magnanimity. Like all the great salesmen he had ever met in his life, the egg woman seemed to have recognized early on that he couldn't be won over by reason, especially since there wasn't any good reason for him to buy what she was selling. So she had taken the only other effective course available to her, which was to talk at him until he gave in, until he told himself he would do anything to stop her incessant looping jabber.

"All right," Eastman said, relieved that their little game was over, "let's see your fucking showroom," and the egg woman, who was already off her toadstool, pushed open the door to her room and he followed her inside, the door swinging pneumatically shut behind them.

It took his eyes a while to adjust, but even then he couldn't see very well—the Snow White drapes were lined with a fabric that didn't let much light through, and the only other window was behind the closed door of the bathroom. This unfortunately heightened his remaining senses, mainly smell—the odor in the room was foul from four or five different sources, though he could isolate only two of them: urine and feces.

The egg woman turned on the TV as if it were a lamp and let her weight sink into the bed. Eastman could see now a pile of turds by the bathroom door and what looked like a snow shovel leaning up against the wall next to it. A little rat of a dog—more head than anything else, Eastman thought—was staring up at him with a limbless, gnaw-marked Barbie doll clenched in its mouth. At first he thought the dog had a bad case of the shakes, but then he realized it was just the ripple effect from its tail, which was wagging magnificently despite the heavy, stench-filled air it was having to displace.

"Goddamnit, Maury," the egg woman said without looking up from a tackle box that she had opened on her lap. "No goddamn fetchee."

On the TV a well-kept host in a yellow sports jacket exhorted the studio audience to remain quiet. The dog dropped the Barbie at its feet and lay down on the soiled carpet with one eye still on Eastman as though it expected him at any moment to snatch at its prize.

"Don't tell me, " Eastman said. "Maury's a dog."

"Well, he ain't no frigging panda bear," the egg woman said, and picked a tiny blue vial out of the tackle box, which she watched for a moment by the crass and shifting light of the picture tube. "How bout a little Ecstasy?" she asked. "That'll put the legs back on ya, at least for a couple of hours." She held up the vial for Eastman's inspection as though she believed he could accurately judge the potency of its contents merely by looking at them, and then let it roll back down her hand into its little partition.

"What else do you have?"

"What direction are you looking for?"

"How many directions are there?"

"Up, down, and sideways. Or if you really got the bug, we got some E-ticket Fantasyland, straight outa the goddamn sixties."

On her palm she displayed what looked like a roll of oversize stamps, only without any printing on them, save for a tiny purple dot at each center.

"That sounds right," Eastman said, affecting confidence, which he thought might elicit a reaction. But the egg woman, as usual, wouldn't flinch.

"How many?" she asked.

"Just one."

"Ten dollars," she said and tore a square of paper off the roll.

"I thought the first one was free?"

"Anything else, we give out samples. What you picked, for a radish like you?—hell, you might never pass this way again."

They sat tableaued in their respective roles while the studio audience clapped indefinitely beneath fast-moving credits. Finally Eastman realized that the egg woman wouldn't budge again until he had offered up his payment, like this video stripper he had seen once in a bar before his accident who took her clothes off a quarter at a time. He wheeled up against the egg woman's bed and handed her the ten, which she silently placed in the bottom of her tackle box, and then set the hit of witch-doctory on the spread by her side. Where before she had seemed acidly maternal, now she seemed remote and without humor, as though all of her patter had been just that—an elaborate form of taking payment and nothing more.

Eastman picked up the little swatch of paper and then looked down at Maury, who was sitting up again with his Barbie; he seemed to understand that the human business was now over and that his chances for playing fetch had dramatically improved.

"So you'll tell everyone," Eastman said, and the egg woman, without speaking, without seeming to think, lifted her hand to the television and changed it to another channel.

There was a little intake of breath after the fourth ring, a kind of sigh that Eastman recognized as the anxious moment preceding Margaret's dialogue with machines of every denomination, and he knew right then she wasn't home (she simply wasn't the type to screen her calls), even before her recorded, too-forthright voice, without identifying itself, implored the person on the line to please leave a message. The significance of the fourth ring did not escape him: he knew that his was the first call since she'd last been home to check her mes-

sages, probably the night before, or that she had re-
trieved the messages from wherever she was now,
probably at work, and that even if there *had* been a
message for her to retrieve, it probably wouldn't
have been personal. So the world has come down
to this, he thought—even a mechanical device
could reveal a person's social score without her
necessarily knowing it—and then the second tone,
the end bracket of *his* message, sounded, and without meaning to, he had left behind mutterings and
erratic breathing as the lone symptoms of his ongoing existence.

He lay on his bed in the dark, thinking he
should call her back, just to explain that it was he,
her brother, Frank, who had left the previous message. But then he thought it was better to leave
things as they were; better she think a nut case had
left his sickness all over her machine than for him
to say whatever reparations had to be said, which
in fact couldn't be said, not in the minute allotted.
At least a crazy person's message was personal,
Eastman thought, even if he did dial his numbers
by chance. Crazy people attached significance to

whatever they perceived; there really wasn't such a thing as chance to them. *Everything* meant something, and as a consequence they meant everything they said. Crazy people had conviction, Eastman realized, which was more than he could say he possessed at the moment, more than he'd possessed for a long, long time, when he really truly thought about it. But here he was thinking again, despite Jarvis's warning to the contrary. Margaret had warned him against pretty much the same thing— or had it been the opposite?—don't sleepwalk through life, she'd told him in that hokey voice of hers, which of course was impossible since he couldn't even fucking walk. He was disabled. Offline. He had long ago accepted that. And yet he had still managed to make a purchase. He had committed after all, even if he didn't quite believe yet in the product. Unfortunately the word on the street didn't travel very fast—the egg woman had no way of broadcasting it except by her large and well-proportioned mouth, which was closed now for the day—and even if she did use her phone, would the likes of Earthling, who he imagined was just stirring now in his little hole beneath the bridge, really have the means to receive it?

No, Eastman told himself, his face forming out of habit into a hollow smirk, he would have to save himself for the time being. He would have to become a man of action, or of limited action, any little thing to keep the plot moving, because the plot was what mattered. Whatever it took to mindlessly pull you through to the next scene, to force you to react to new stimuli. Even if the nerve was dead, you had to keep hitting it with one of those little hammers the doctors used, keep checking it for twitch, keep feeling around for it with the part of you that still could; you would stop breathing otherwise. Your lungs would simply seize up on you. So what if Moonier hadn't really used a straw to accomplish *his* breathing? A needle wasn't all that different when you really got right down to it. Maybe the boat inside really was the ticket. If you believed you were traveling, wasn't that the same as actually doing it?

Eastman opened his hands and held them out from himself as if they were a scale. He wanted to feel the weight of the little piece of paper in his hand, but no matter how hard he concentrated, he couldn't get a sense of it. Of course, this whole rap of Jarvis's was probably bullshit; his interest in this scheme, whatever it was, was probably much clearer than he had made it out to be. And probably the only thing that this undetectable substance in his hand would insure was his permanent insanity. But what did that matter? In a year or two the very space he was occupying would in all likelihood be a part of some exotic new ride, with long lines of weary tourists leading up to its new and measured terror. Maybe if he were still alive at the time of its construction, he could hurl himself into the wet concrete like some martyred worker on the Hoover Dam. Except, of course, he wouldn't even be able to hoist himself up on the scaffolding to pull off such a stunt—Jarvis was right about that part of it, even if the rest *was* bullshit: there was simply no point in speculating about the future. The probability of any one event transpiring was the number of possible events stacked against it; everything that happened was by its nature a fluke.

Once something had taken place, no matter how twisted, you couldn't explain it away. The whole trick was to abandon the notion of cause and effect. You wouldn't have the fortitude to deal with things as they were until you did.

But why did he have to convince himself of this now? he wondered, turning over on his side. Isn't this what he had believed in since his accident?

He heard a noise in the bathroom and his mind abruptly stalled with panic: he listened for several minutes to odd tickings and what he ultimately determined to be his dripping faucet. Then just as suddenly he burst into laughter, or more a child's sustained *hee*—he was already imagining things and he hadn't even taken the drug yet.

He closed his eyes, then lifted the swatch of paper to his mouth and placed it on his tongue, the way Jarvis had his strawberry, and began to gently suck on it. He couldn't detect any flavor other than the same bitter aftertaste that he experienced whenever the dentist X-rayed his teeth. Then he swallowed and the paper vanished into his body, and he lay as he had before, trying desperately not to think. He had never really experimented with anything like this, outside of a couple puffs of marijuana, which had only succeeded in making him sleepy. But that was before his accident, when he was still a member of the enabled himself, before he had really ever thought about anything. He was still a member of the audience back then. He was still clapping and booing at the same bogus program right along with the rest of them. Maybe this Fantasyland, as the egg woman called it, would counteract all the weirdness that had been accumulating in him since. They gave uppers to hyperactive children, didn't they? Maybe this ticket, this boat inside, operated by the same perverse logic. Once this Fantasyland had kicked in, he would be on autopilot: all the necessary motivation would be provided for him. He would finally have that psycho's conviction, at least for a few hours (the egg woman had all but guaranteed it), and by the time the drug had worn off, the new word on the street would be in effect. He would be a part of the system then—at last he would belong here—

and from that point on, his addiction to the mystery would be formalized; they could mail his disability to the egg woman directly for all he would care, or even to a P.O. box in Disneyland. That was all there was to it. Maybe someday he and Earthling would even go on the road to Bali together, side-kicks in a foreign land.

"Just like Hope and Crosby," he muttered and compelled his mouth into a smile.

The transition was the only tricky part, East-man advised himself, remembering that his ex-roommate had called this awkward little space between sobriety and intoxication the moment of doubt. If you fought against it, your body would go one way, your mind another. You had to ease into this thing. You had to be mellow. Then you'd be riding the wild surf before you knew what hit you. Then you'd be delivered. It was exactly as Earth-ling had called it: release *was* release, and it didn't matter if you released yourself or if the world was released upon you. In the end, the effect was ex-actly the same.

"Don't think," Eastman said aloud, "don't fuck-

ing think," and then he reached blindly for the remote control on the nightstand and began to
randomly press buttons. In another moment the
picture tube ignited and he was watching the
black-and-white image of a man not much older
than himself—or at least when the footage had
been shot—taking a bottle of Coca-Cola from a
wooden case on the floor of somebody's very clean
garage. The man had just opened the bottle and
begun swigging from it, when another man, whom
Eastman recognized as the star of the show, blun-
dered onto the scene. "Why don't you help yourself, Thorny?" the star asked the first man, who
looked sheepishly toward the camera, and from
there the lighthearted banter escalated until some
flimsy plot line involving an outboard motor had
moved the scene to an auction hall.

The basso profundo chortle of someone in the
laugh track cleaved to Eastman's mind, even after he
had changed channels, so he changed back again and
tried to watch the show as he had as a child, when,
as he recalled it now, he and Margaret had made
it part of their Saturday night watching schedule.

But he couldn't find any humor in the shifting
scenes, and, in fact, after a time he couldn't figure
out anymore where he was supposed to laugh—the
canned titters and clappings had begun to spray out
into the room like shrapnel. He pressed the button
marked VOLUME and watched an unnatural green
line of hash marks shrink into nothing, and then the
miming image of a teenaged boy stared out at him
from the convex glass, his hair crew-cut and oiled,
with two short wands of it sticking from behind his
ears like the eyes from a closeted potato. Eastman
flashed that this was the star's son, in real life *and* in
the show, and that the star and his wife were also
playing themselves, and that years later, after acting
out his adolescence in front of millions of total
strangers, the son had married and had a son of his
own, which had also been incorporated into the
show, with *his* wife ultimately playing *herself,* right
along with the rest of them. Eastman remembered
now that it was these episodes, of the two bickering
newlyweds playing out their pathetic little lives,
that he and Margaret had watched on Saturdays,
and that it was reruns of the much earlier episodes

that they'd watched after school in the same years, though he didn't remember this seeming at all peculiar to him at the time. It was later, he recalled now, after the show had been canceled and he was in the midst of his own adolescence, that in real life the couple had messily divorced, though for once without any televised counterpart. Eventually the son had OD'd on some fashionable drug of the time, and Eastman wondered where the rest of the principals were now, assuming any of them were still alive. No doubt living on their residual money in some sequestered hell, he told himself—helpless, just like he was, in the face of actual existence.

"Fucking history," he said, and closed his hand into a fist before watching it go limp again. Fucking television history. This wasn't the way it was supposed to work. He didn't need to pay money to trip on what he already knew, on what, in fact, he wanted to forget—he did that all the time anyway. She owes me a fucking refund, he told himself, and then suddenly it was obvious that the egg woman had sold him a bill of goods, that she was probably sitting in her room this very moment with Maury in her lap, ingesting her thousandth episode of "Wheel of Fortune" while she marked another roll of empty stamps with a purple felt pen. Fantasyland is what she saved for gringos like himself—that's why she didn't hand out free samples of it: she wouldn't be able to cheat anyone that way. Fraud within fraud within fraud. You got fantasy when you ordered reality, reality when you ordered fantasy. Except the lines weren't nearly that clean. Blurry lines—that's what all these fuckers traded in. And even if you could ever prove they'd been ripping you off, which enabled agency would you report it to? The police? The FBI? Or better yet, why not some glib consumer ombudsman on the local news? That way you could watch your own pathetic bullshit along with the rest of the tripping saps.

"Loops," he said. The whole thing ran in loops. It just wouldn't hold still long enough for you to see it.

Channels had been flashing for quite some time on the bed between his upturned legs, when with one hand he removed the other from the re-

mote. All of the transmitted light had accumulated
in the telephone, which was ringing loudly and
coarsely, linking up with cold, crisp apples in his
mind. He rode the harmonics along their own little
paths for a while, then tuned back into the main
tone, which seemed organic now and blaring, like
someone whining through a bullhorn.

He took the phone up in his hand and squeezed
it between the mattress and the deadened small of
his back, then grooved that the drapes were pulled
open and the little white cat was sitting at the entrance to its den—they shared eyes and it was wanting to play, that was the zone of it, the play zone,
and it went like that for a while until he pulled his
hand out from underneath himself and it was atoms
in a hive, eddies in a place, and he watched the
blood go back into it, inflating his fingers, turning
them against the light, watching them lift up the receiver and press the square buttons as he waited for
the message from inside the black shell.

"Right, right," he said, his lips against the stip-
pled plastic, reading it with tongue. "Ear, man," and
swiveled the dangled end of it up to the rest of his

head, pushing it onto fleshy bone. There were singers now where the TV was, black chicks loose in a strident glow—mouths moved in one place, sound came out another: *hold on to your love you got to hold on to your love you got to*

"City, please."

"Slimp," he said. "Slimptown. New fucking Slimp."

Be cool, baby. You're all right now, baby. Everything in its own little place.

"What city, please?"

"I don't know, please," speaking lightly to a knuckle. Other hand now, baby. In its own little place. "I don't know where she's at," he said, this time to the phone. "Violet Slimp. Like in shrimp. Do you know where you're at? It's not such an easy question."

"I have a Chance on Coronet Circle—please hold for the number."

Got nowhere else to go, sweetheart. Might as well hold onto you.

Earwise, he was in a groove with black chicks, with a drum machine, with numbers sequenced in a manufactured voice. The rest of it was the little white cat, posing now, pointing with its skeleton tail, jerking it like a scorpion. Like it was on a fucking string! *hold on to your love you got to hold* Then he was cool again for a second, turning his head from the cat, which was just now burying its freshly rendered dung.

"Once again," the telephone informed him, and this time the black chicks took what were left of his senses, filling him with accents, with wiggles, with wordless incantations.

When next he saw himself in space, he was boxing his ear with the receiver. He pounded the remote with his free hand until it broke down the cycle, until the room was black and he was lying facedown on the mattress, his arms held tight against his sides. "One piece," he said, "you got to be one piece, baby," to which the telephone replied, "Please hang up and try again." Then he was holding the receiver to his mouth, breathing from it as though it dispensed a precious gas. He looped back to the operator, who was asking him for the city, her voice bouncing in and out of his ear.

"Loops," he told her. "Loopsburg. Mr. Slimp lives there. Mr. S-L-I-M-P. Same place you live, honey. Same place as all this."

This time he was ready when the synthetic femme came on, the number etching like a mantra onto permanent memory. He spoke the number loudly into the room, laughing hard after each digit, then scrambled it a few times before putting it back together again, his fingers acting out the numbers on the keypad. The little white cat was with him on this: it was doing its cat thing, swimming in dirt, rolling around like a stabbed bull. It was all just play. The word on the street said *play*.

"Let us play," he said into the phone, and rolled off the mattress. His temple struck the wooden leg of the nightstand on the way down, and he saw the pain in the back of his eyes, a whole sun's worth, shining on the screen. Then it was the shag of the point-blank rug, the motion of the fibers as they blended into sight. His mouth flexed against the carpet, but no words, and then his head rocked back over, surfacing in air.

"Brain surgery," he announced, above the tide of his room, then tracked the circuitry of his face into a smile. He saw now that the thing fed into itself: seeing how a smile came together caused a mouth to turn up that way.

"Fucking loops," he said into the phone, "fucking grinny-face loops."

Then he was cramping, his lips in a coil, the skin on his face drawn tight over his skull. You-are-going-to-make-it, came little bytes of Violet, while little shards of paint were flaking off the ceiling, catching in the fractured porchlight, mixing with the tiny prophesies of dust that inhabited the room. He was sucking all of it into his lungs. It was filling him up, weighing him down. He was tortoise meat now. He was belly-up to the rare and common elements.

Quick, shallow rabbit breaths gave way to a scream. The half of him that still could raised itself and then everything drained out of him for the moment. He was looking at the telephone, which was off the hook, resting on the carpet by his thigh: it was spitting tacks into the air, little noisy tacks in the same relentless beat. He picked it up and lay it precisely in its anchored cradle. All he wanted now was his money back, plain and simple. He was more *here* at the moment than he ever had been, ever wanted to be. Where was the vacation in that? he wondered, and saw the Medusa head of Earthling poke like a puppet from behind the bathroom door.

"What you think is what you get," he advised the room, which was divvied up now among billions of autonomous pixels. He looked again at the spot where Earthling's cartoon head had appeared and saw it was aboil with nothingness. No being could take form in such a place, he reassured himself, or at least for any length of time. This notion chilled him until the schematic of his own impossible machine surfaced in his mind. He watched his hand flex and unflex in innumerable discrete phases—synapse-muscle-sinew-bone—each time seeing new, intermediate steps, until it took all his powers of concentration just to point his finger at the ceiling. Then he flashed on the Rube Goldberg apparatus of his heart and lungs, felt the weight of consciousness slow them down and speed them up; his whole body was in opposing shudders and he was removing his clothes, which were suffocating him, which were keeping the nutrients in the speckled air from reaching his enlarged and gasping pores. He flailed on the carpet for quite some time before he was equal again, and then his hand was holding doorknob, grooving to the cool surface of the metal, to the whole reality of surfaces, which had all at once returned to him, in Technicolor spades.

The seal was broken. The night air lifted him up, propping him against the narrow rectangle of the door's edge.

"Naked in ether," he declared, and the cat, dagger-tongued and licking itself at the center of the pool, flashed him its permanent smile. Everything was elegantly contrived now, lit from within, shining in a warp of candy-coated space. He pulled himself across the courtyard on his stomach, all the while keeping a bead on the cat, which ran into its hiding place once he'd reached the edge of the pool. He followed after it a few more feet before sparks began shooting into the corners of his eyes and he could feel his lungs and heart beating once more out of rhythm. He lifted his head up until it snagged on the immovable cane of his spine, and then all at once he saw that he was alone, that he was cornered in a horribly dark and cramped place.

He opened his mouth to yell, but he didn't have any breath; the rats were all over him, crawling over his back, burrowing themselves between his body and the cold, dry earth, and then they were inside him, pushing down his windpipe, gouging through his tightened veins. He flailed, trying to expel them, crawling, rolling, begging, and when he finally gave up, he was lying, still naked, on his back in the planter outside the motel, in full view of the indifferent traffic.

His neck was folded up against some obstacle. He coiled all his strength into his shoulders and pulled downward on his head until his body lay flat on the ground and he was staring up the barrel of a luminous palm tree, its preposterous length extending far into the darkness above him. He was reliving the moment after he had fallen, a moment, he realized now, of exacting purity. The before of

himself had been compressed by forces more powerful and invisible than gravity into this single
shiny widget of present; he closed his mind around
it, savoring its textures, like a child fondling a silver
dollar. How could such an event be so cleanly
imagined, he wondered, so literally a transforma-
tion? How could a person move in the speed of
light from a life not lived to a death not died, in
such a seamless loop of folly and inconsequence?

He lay marveling at the cruel symmetry of the
thing until he saw that he was trapped inside of it,
until he saw that he was the thing itself and would
remain, like a grain of sand, in this one innocuous
shape forever. The loop was spinning so fast he'd
become a still photograph of himself, his body not
a corpse, but a Polaroid of a corpse, tossed in the
weeds with the gum wrappers and the butts of cig-
arettes. He wanted to cry out, to ventilate his pain,
to protest his undeserved fate, but there was no
room for it in the picture. Instead his panic remained sealed inside him, ebbing and surging until
it had eroded his nerves and he lay ravaged by his
own immobile condition.

He closed his eyes then and saw himself exposed to the unfeeling universe, but he had no feeling of his own—the picture merely showed him as he was—and in the next instant, sleep overtook him, thick and dreamless, like a dose of anesthetic shot directly into his veins.

There was no thought to precede the opening of Eastman's eyes—there was nothing, utter blackness, and then the sky, gray and misty, coloring the unbuffered cities beneath him in a half-made light. The world was no longer in a state of flux; it was literally sideways now—he was looking at it through a white-painted railing, his head laid, it seemed to him precisely, on a bed of well-tended lawn. Even the airplanes, a few of which he could see in a far-off distance, seemed suspended forever in the airy depths. Then he saw that one of them was moving, it was lowering itself through the sky, and he understood that he was witnessing a holding pattern—the planes were queued up to make their final descents.

"Get on with it," he told them, and was surprised to hear his own voice working, surprised his
ears could perceive it, his brain could understand
it. He reached over his shoulder and felt a blanket
draped over himself, then moved his hand underneath it and felt his naked body, running his fingers
along the cool surface of his skin until it seemed he
was feeling someone else's. He pinched his left
thigh for a long time after this, waiting for the pain,
for some aura of the pain, to register in his mind.
But there was none. In the background he heard
what sounded like a waterfall, a little one, and behind it, the intermittent notes of a guitar. Someone
was singing intermittently as well—there was no
mistaking the twang.

He rolled over on his back and looked around
him, his eyes swiveling in his head like a chame-
leon's; everywhere he saw bonsai trees and stone
lanterns, all in suspended orbit around an immense
house of blue-tiled gables and elaborate cornices—
he seemed to be on the grounds of some new-
fangled Japanese mansion. Then he met the frozen
gaze of a huge calcified Buddha that was sitting on

a wooden deck attached to the house—though when he looked closer, he saw that its eyes, set above its ambiguous smile, were, in fact, closed. He stared at it in a kind of trance anyway, until he had to shut his own eyes again, to shield them from the glary, diffused light.

"Where is this?" he called out, in as loud a voice as he could muster, and after a small wait the music stopped, and Eastman lifted his head to look out over his covered body, across the expansive lawn to some sort of garden whose inner sanctum was concealed from him by a row of Japanese pines. Then he noticed a little bridge spanning a garden pool that acted as a line of sight to Violet: she was sitting in a wooden deck chair with her guitar resting on its arms, staring into nothing, or into something that he wasn't able to see. In the next moment she rose easily and began walking barefoot toward him across the bridge, though as if she had no particular destination, as if she were strolling for its own sake, without having heard him call. A breeze came up suddenly then, winding her loose-fitting calico dress around her limber form, and it seemed that her guitar, which she was holding precariously by the neck, was the only thing keeping her on the ground.

When she finally reached him, she sat down cross-legged on the grass by his side and stared blankly at him for a minute or so, like a doctor viewing her infant patient. Then, with the prognosis apparently to her liking, she broke into her much-dimpled smile.

Eastman recognized the sequence, though without any sense of dread. She had used the same routine on him that first day in the airport.

"Welcome to Chez Chance," she told him, the smile quickly dissolving into her unreadable deadpan. "I hope you don't mind, but I thought you should sleep under the stars, the few of them we have left. You seemed to want to be outdoors, anyway, and, well, you know Howard. He doesn't allow me to bring anybody inside anymore. I didn't figure you'd get in too much trouble out here—he's got the whole place rigged with alarms. He even has a little electric fence around the koi pond, to keep out the raccoons, he says. A coon's a lot nastier than you are, so I didn't figure you for drowning. Besides, you were pretty much in one place by the time I found you."

He was enjoying her voice as he would music, without focusing on any of the particulars. He closed his eyes, hoping she would oblige him with more. The breeze crept across him like a shadow. He wanted her to tell him a story.

"You called me last night, Frank, do you remember? I guess you were really calling Howard, but I picked up the phone. At first I thought maybe it was somebody touched, I was hearing so many spoons, but then I recognized your voice. Were you calling for help, Frank? That's how I took it. Howard wasn't here, so I drove the Cadillac—I know where he keeps the keys—and when I got to your motel, there you were, Frank, naked as a jaybird in them Christmas lights and no one batting an eye. So I gathered you up and went to get your things, and there was this boy with ropy hair in your room—his hair was like one of those court jester hats, only it didn't have no bells on it—and he was trying on some of your clothes, Frank. He was wearing your pants and thumbing through your traveler's checks, smiling at them like they was a deck of pretty cards. Soon as he got a whiff of me, it was a whole different story—he actually hissed at me, Frank—he opened his mouth and tried to breathe fire on me, but nothing came out, and then he just beat it out of there.

"Do you think maybe he swallowed the same pill as you? That's what I figured anyhow. In my whole life I never seen anything like it. Moonier had a bent for roller coasters, but at least his ran on tracks. Whatever it was, it seemed like you got your money's worth."

He heard her sigh. He heard her gust like a moment of long-awaited breeze. Then he heard her pick out a few notes on her guitar.

"I'm writing a song about you, Frank—a fast little waltz. It's going to be real upbeat."

Eastman opened his eyes again and looked at Violet, who was studying her hand, in chord formation, on the neck of her guitar. He couldn't tell if she was kidding or not, though he realized that it didn't matter to him one way or another. Then he heard a glass door sliding over its aluminum track, and when he turned his head once more to face the house, he saw a groggy-looking Chance, in a pair of white socks and an oversized kimonolike bathrobe, step from behind the sand-colored drapes and walk purposefully to the deck's rail, over which he spat a mouthful of amber liquid into the gravel beneath him. He stared after it a moment as though willing the earth to accept his latest discharge, then lifted his face to look thoughtfully at Violet.

"You forgot to cover up its head," he told his sister, then rubbed each of his eyes with opposing index fingers. "You and the corpus delicti will be leaving today, won't you, Violet? I can't afford to be involved in any more of your criminal activities."

Eastman tried sitting up for a moment but suddenly could no longer see the point of it. Instead he looked above him at Chance, who, by the first, dim light of morning, still had a weird polish about him, though balanced against his disheveled appearance, he seemed to be playing a role that came naturally to him—that of an unceremonious master of ceremonies.

"I would just as soon not be here," Eastman announced.

"Death speaks," Chance said. "How artistic."

"He was only going to spend the one night," Violet said.

"And then be on his merry way?" said Chance. "He doesn't seem to have his wheelchair anymore, Vi. Why is it that everyone you try to rescue winds up more helpless because of it?"

"Maybe I should scramble us some eggs," Violet said. "I saw some of those curly fries in the deep freeze."

"Yes," Chance said, "and we could sit down together in the breakfast nook and break bread with one another, just like civilized people. Just like a family," he said, and clasped his hands together in a melodramatic way. "Except now Frank here seems to be a quadriplegic, Vi. Sitting seems beyond him at this point. But maybe we could stretch him out right on the kitchen table, huh? That way he wouldn't have to bother coping with a chair."

By some reflex he had wholly forgotten, Eastman sat up, this time without faltering, and the

blanket fell away from his chest; the damp morning air seemed to condense immediately on his
bare skin, causing him to shiver. He looked over at
Violet, who was in her same cross-legged position
on the grass, only now she had a distant and child-
like smile on her face. He remembered seeing the
same expression on a cop one Fourth of July, his
first in L.A.—she was wearing a bulletproof vest
and eating a large ice-cream cone.

He turned back to Chance now, expecting
somehow to see the same tranquilized look, but
Chance was staring right at him, his eyes keen, his
mouth sharply frowning.

"You really are an asshole," Eastman told him.

"But I'm so much more than that," Chance
replied, and then his eyes took back their familiar
sheen, as if he were once again addressing a much
larger and more gullible audience. "I have hair and
teeth and skin and bones. I have *legs*. I have a job.
And to my clientele, I *have* to be nice. I have to ap-
plaud their neuroses in three dimensions, admire
their choice of this twenty thousand square feet
over that twenty thousand square feet. The smart

ones—and most of them are—know they're being stroked and they don't care, because that's what they pay their money for, to see their little monkey crank its organ."

Chance moved his head slowly, like a lizard eyeing a bug, until he was staring directly at Eastman again with the same impervious scowl. "But you, Frank, you're *my* monkey. It's my unconscionable tax outlay that subsidizes your pathetic existence. You don't even have a fucking organ, for chrissakes. I don't *have* to be nice to you."

Now Chance smiled in the same distracted way as the Buddha sitting behind him, the same way as Violet and the ice-cream–eating cop, and Eastman could see there was no sense in doing battle with him; if need be, he would use every card in his long and impeccably stacked deck.

"So what do you think of the decor?" Chance asked, and spread out his upturned hands to indicate the massive grounds, his bathrobe sagging from his arms like two ill-formed and useless wings. "Personally I think it's really tacky, but the seller—well, this was his version of heaven. Can you imagine spending eternity in this place?" He laughed abruptly and loudly, as though at a client's not very funny and off-color joke, then just as quickly sobered again. "The guy was a builder by occupation—he threw up all sorts of crappy developments down *there*—but this one here was his baby. He said he built it as a memorial to some geisha girl he met in Japan just after the surrender, back when he was still a soldier. He had this whole rap down about her, how they were supposed to get married, and then how she died—'tragically,' as he put it. He never did explain what offed her. She must've given one hell of a blow job, that's all I have to say. I could tell it really chapped his Wonderbread wife, the whole goddamn shrine aspect of the place, but I'm sure he had paid dearly for her silence, just as he had the two or three wives previous—though it couldn't have been more than what he ultimately paid for mine. I mean, the guy spent years putting this heap together, which of course he felt obligated to tell me about in every pathetic detail. You have to admit it is ghastly in a million inspired ways. This place is the work of an accom-

plished hack, don't you think? The guy actually
called this place his canvas, if you can believe that.
And you should've seen the look on his face when
he signed the papers—you'd swear I'd leveraged
him out of the Taj Mahal. What an idiot. He
should've thought of that before he built a fifty-
unit condo park in the middle of a recession. His
timing was for shit, that's all.

"I wasn't even planning to buy the place, really.
On paper it just didn't look like much, even at the
fire-sale price. But as soon as I got up here, I started
warming to the idea. The whole thing went off in
my head, like it was all a pretty dream: first I take it
off the seller's hands for next to nothing, then I
wait a few months, set my price artificially high,
and then I reel in the next nouveau riche with bad
taste, which is like ninety-nine out of a hundred.
That's why the seller was having such a hard time
moving it—he wasn't asking nearly enough! I mean
this place is custom, man. So what if it's custom
bullshit, the point is it's some sick fucker's sick
dream of a house, which means it's some other sick
fucker's dream house, 'cause those are the cats with

all the money, the sick fuckers, and they all think they're original in the same fucked-up way. When rich cats fall asleep, they all watch the same shitty channel.

"But I wasn't about to tell the seller any of that. We were in negotiation, after all—that's just not part of the routine. As a matter of fact, the guy didn't even know I was *in* negotiation, that's how cool I was about the whole deal, which was really too bad for him. That's what he gets for trying to save the commission: you try selling without an agent, it winds up costing you a lot more in the end.

"So after one of the longest hours of my life, the guy wraps up his cornball tour of the place, and I'm starting to walk, right? I'm starting to check my planner for my next appointment, as though I *have* a next appointment, when the guy starts going into *his* routine: how he's had this place on the market for practically a year, how pretty soon he'll have to file bankruptcy, how he's spent his entire adult life building a monument and now he has to sell it for a quarter of its worth just so he can put his kids through fancy Eastern schools. On and on and on. The guy is practically whining about his six-hundred-large-a-year lifestyle, and my heart is leaking like a goddamn pasta sieve, it really is. The blood is seeping through my goddamn Pierre Cardin shirt.

"But you know what finally clinches it?—not the sob story about his geisha nooky, not the maxed-out gold card or the no-refund ticket to Chapter Nine—it's that the guy throws in all his crappy belongings. Can you imagine? All the tacky Jap art and Buddhas and rattan whatever. All the goddamn Fujiyama neckties. If I have one piece of advice, that would be it: when a man offers to throw in his bathrobe, whip out your checkbook—that's when you know you've found his best price."

For a moment Chance stood basking in the glow of his own self-generated light—it was as if he were waiting for a thunderous applause to subside—then focused again on Eastman, who was watching him as he might a television.

"Now I own this baby free and clear," Chance said, beaming. "And I'm in escrow for three times what I paid for it. But these woods are just about tapped out now. When they put the next strip of papier-mâché on *this* mountain, the whole thing is gonna collapse. You'll be able to see the cloud of dust for miles, just like another Hiroshima. Of course, I'll be way out of sight by then. The market's moving north, and I'm moving with it—Montana, Idaho, that's where the gold is now. There ain't much riffraff up there, and what little there is of it gets killed off by the winters. It's this back-to-nature trip everybody's into these days—you know, survival of the goddamn fittest. Personally, I prefer the warm weather, but you can't let that get in the way of business. Besides, I plan on having my nest egg put together by the time it goes bust up there. Then I'll retire offshore, do a Brando and buy myself a little tropical fiefdom. I plan on having *able*-bodied servants to wait on me, Frank, a whole shitload of them, and I won't be paying dime one in fucking taxes."

He smiled now, almost giddily, his eyes staring deeply into Eastman's. "What I'm trying to point out to you, Frank, is that this is your lucky day. You just hit the goddamn mother of all lottos. I'm bequeathing the whole kit-and-caboodle, the whole

goddamn county—hell, the whole goddamn state—
what's left of it, anyway—to you and the rest of
your parasite buddies. I wish I could stick around
to watch the show, Frank. All those tapeworms in
the same little jar would really be something to see.
That's the problem with working for a living—you
miss half the good stuff. I guess you can't have
everything."

He suddenly trotted down the steps leading to
the yard and then disappeared around an angle of
the house before returning with an empty wheelbarrow that he pushed up to the spot where Eastman was lying, the front tire coming to rest against
a wedge of Eastman's stomach. "Help me out with
this, Vi," he told his sister, and without voicing an
objection, almost as if she were responding to an
emergency, she rose from her trancelike state to as-
sist him. Eastman didn't say anything either as they
wrapped him in the blanket and lifted him into the
wheelbarrow, then pushed him roughly down a
pebbled walk to the garage, where they loaded him
into Chance's Mercedes and shut the door, the car,
as it sealed him in, expelling a vacuum hush of air.

Eastman watched, but couldn't hear, them ex-change a few terse words before they moved into the house, and in another five minutes they reap-peared with blank faces, Violet sliding Eastman's suitcase onto his lap and then sliding herself onto the seat next to him, her own luggage stacked pre-cariously on her peaked knees, while Chance, still in his white socks and acquired bathrobe, assumed his position behind the wheel.

They drove in a stoic's silence, as if being towed to their destination, down a labyrinth of wide stop-sign-and-peopleless streets, passing among large new estates that were boxy derivations of sundry archi-tectural styles, all packed haphazardly together—a Swiss chalet; a Spanish villa; a Greek mansion; a replica of a Frank Lloyd Wright. This went on for what seemed like miles, until they reached a gate with a small guard station, where a man resembling Eastman's father, only in uniform, waved them into the world at large using a nod and a grim smile.

They crossed their first avenue to where the trees were larger and much greater in number and the curbs and sidewalks had given way to gently

molded streets and low-slung ranch houses set way
back in their lots, homes that, in another era, had
kept the prosperous, but in this new and nameless
age, disparaged themselves with their own tired
brand of modesty. Soon, too, this neighborhood
faded into another; here the homes were also rem-
nants of prosperity, though from a previous age:
they were primarily Victorian mansions, divided
now into apartments and allowed to fall into various states of disrepair; cars were parked on many of
the once expansive lawns, and small clumps of
mostly young and Hispanic men had congregated
on some of the porches, staring out with a hostile
indifference at the commuters who were driving
swiftly past.

In another few blocks they had reached the
base of the hill and a new assortment of gaudily
presented franchise businesses, much like the area
surrounding Disneyland. Chance pulled up to a
bus stop in front of a gas station, and with the car
still running, he and Violet carried Eastman, his
suitcase balanced on his stomach, to the bench and
propped him up on it.

"Happy foraging," Chance told Eastman, then turned to give Violet the same perfunctory hug that he'd used to greet her at the airport.

When she had been released, Violet looked at her brother without any visible sentiment. "How will I find you?" she asked him.

"You always do," Chance said and stared for a brief moment down the interminable boulevard as though charting his escape. Then he got in his car and drove away.

They sat for quite a while not saying anything after that, the morning commute anointing their silence with Doppler-shifted car noises. The traffic had thinned out considerably when the first bus finally came, but Violet waved it on, and Eastman looked over at her for the first time since they'd been deposited there by Chance: she had on a guilt-wracked expression, though Eastman noticed almost right away that her brow was *too* furrowed, her eyes *too* sunken—she'd had too much time to work on her pose.

"Where to from here?" she asked, and briefly made eye contact with Eastman, her dour look filming over with a tepid smile. "I've got a gig up in Missoula next week. They're not paying my way there like this last job did, but it's still work. I was going to ride a Greyhound until you called. Now I thought maybe we could rent a car. I know you're no stranger to travel."

She opened up her guitar case, and from inside a yellow velveteen pocket she extracted Eastman's traveler's checks, which she tossed onto his blanketed lap. "There's over four hundred dollars there," she said, and jacked up her smile. "We could buy you a little wardrobe and still have enough left over for a vacation, a small one, anyway. We could have ourselves a time, Frank. What do you say? Our bus will be here any second."

"No," Eastman said with all of Chance's resolve, though that was the only word he could manage.

"All right then," said Violet instantly, as though she'd expected him to reject her offer all along. But what little color was in her face had drained off entirely, and she seemed on the verge of some great sadness. "There's one more thing, Frank," she said. "I didn't have the heart to tell you before. Last night, when I came to pick you up? I couldn't find your wheelchair. I looked all over for it, but I just couldn't find it."

The next bus pulled up then, and she rose to board it, her suitcase and guitar her only ballast. But she stopped as she was halfway up the steps, turning back to give Eastman one last look.

"So you'll just have to walk, you bastard," she said, her voice in the half-step between anger and pleading. "Won't you please, please, please just *walk?*"

The doors of the bus closed behind her, and then she, too, was carried away from him, down the same endless street that had taken Chance.

Eastman sat on the bench staring into the space that Violet had so recently occupied, but her image quickly vanished from it, and he doubted that he would be able to conjure her so easily again. He felt sleep-deprived, unable to hold on to any one of the memories that were currently flooding his mind: he saw his sister and his mother having an argument about what college she would attend; he saw his father playing horseshoes with his drunken

Aunt Caroline; he saw his grandmother on an Easter Sunday, clueing his sister and him to the whereabouts of the last hidden egg. They were average scenes from an average life, he thought. But the images were out of sequence. They followed no pattern that he could discern. He was channel surfing inside his own head.

And the rest of the day went like that, too, the recollections coming and going, interspersed with occasional buses, all of which he motioned onward. In fact, it wasn't until well past dark, when he was exhausted and cold and hungry, that he finally understood the connection: they were scenes from his past, from before his accident, from before everything in his life had turned to this. He was *here* now, wherever here was. His feet were on *this* ground, even if they couldn't feel it. He didn't have to look to make sure that it was true.

So he tried imagining what could be done with the rest of his life, what shape he could will himself into that the rest of the world could imagine. But it was a shape he wasn't able to foresee. When the last bus arrived, it was empty except for a few riders, all of them women, bunched together into two seats near the front. They didn't seem to see Eastman there on the bench below them, or even any world beyond their own, as though they were fish living in the dim and greenish realm of an aquarium. Eastman vowed right then that he would lead a life in whatever disenchanted place this bus finally took him, and when he told the driver that he needed help, she called to her passengers in Spanish, and, tiredly, they carried him aboard.

ABOUT THE AUTHOR

Jay Gummerman is a graduate of the M.F.A. program at the University of California at Irvine. Born in Whittier, California, he lives with his wife, Kelly, in San Clemente. His first book, a collection of short stories, is titled *We Find Ourselves in Moontown.*